I0638045

The Woman in Red

A Sebastian McCabe—Jeff Cody Mystery

ALSO BY DAN ANDRIACCO

The Sebastian McCabe—Jeff Cody Mysteries
No Police Like Holmes
Holmes Sweet Holmes
The 1895 Murder
The Disappearance of Mr. James Phillimore
Rogues Gallery
Bookmarked for Murder
Erin Go Bloody
Queen City Corpse
Death Masque
Too Many Clues
Murderers' Row
No Ghosts Need Apply
The English Garden Mystery

The Enoch Hale Trilogy (with Kieran McMullan)
The Amateur Executioner
The Poisoned Penman
The Egyptian Curse

Sherlock Holmes
Baker Street Beat
House of the Doomed
The Sword of Death

School for Sleuths
School for Sleuths
The Medium Is the Murder

The Woman in Red

A Sebastian McCabe—Jeff Cody Mystery

Dan Andriacco

First edition published in 2023
© Copyright 2023
Dan Andriacco

The right of Dan Andriacco to be identified as the author of this work has been asserted by him in accordance with the Copyright, Designs and Patents Act 1998.

All rights reserved. No reproduction, copy or transmission of this publication may be made without express prior written permission. No paragraph of this publication may be reproduced, copied or transmitted except with express prior written permission or in accordance with the provisions of the Copyright Act 1956 (as amended). Any person who commits any unauthorized act in relation to this publication may be liable to criminal prosecution and civil claims for damage.

All characters appearing in this work are fictitious. Any resemblance to real persons, living or dead, is purely coincidental. The opinions expressed herein are those of the authors and not of MX Publishing.

Paperback ISBN 978-1-80424-325-1
ePub ISBN 978-1-80424-326-8
PDF ISBN 978-1-80424-327-5

Published by MX Publishing
335 Princess Park Manor, Royal Drive,
London, N11 3GX
www.mxpublishing.com
Cover design by Brian Belanger

This one is for
Ann Brauer Andriacco
my woman in red

"I would not wish any companion in the world but you."
—*The Tempest, Act III, Scene 1*

CONTENTS

Chapter One
Red Alert

IT'S NEVER A good sign to come back from lunch and find your lawyer waiting for you.

"Uh-oh," I said, or possibly something stronger.

True, Kelly Jane Richards isn't my personal legal eagle, but she is vice president of compliance risk and legal affairs/general counsel for St. Benignus University. And any mess involving SBU quickly winds up on my plate as head communications honcho (more formally, vice president of marketing and communications) of our little institution.

"She just got here, Boss," said Analiese "Popcorn" Pokorny, my assistant honcho and office sparring partner. This was by way of excuse for not giving my cell a jingle to warn me. From their body language, I figured Richards had been refueling from Popcorn's bottomless tank of campus gossip before I arrived.

I waved the barrister into my office.

"What did I do now, or not do, and how can you get me out of it?" I quipped as she took the chair across from my desk.

"Cute, Jeff," she said, "but not very." Richards is a large woman with big brown eyes, a pretty face, and black hair with a streak of white down the center. Although she parks lawyerly glasses on her head and dresses conservatively in business-like tweeds, she fancies clunky jewelry. Today she wore a necklace with large crimson stones of some kind, maybe jasper. Almost every one of her fingers bore a ring. "Nobody screwed up yet, Jeff, and I'd like to keep it that way. It's not a legal matter, more of a potential PR issue, which is why I darkened your door. I really just wanted to give you a red alert of something that might happen. An early warning."

"I appreciate that, Kelly." *So I can get a head start on worrying.* "What's up?"

She leaned forward. "Rosie Hawthorne told me over chili at Beans & Books this afternoon that she nominated Parker Williams for the Everett P. Chandler Alumni Career Achievement Award. That's not good."

Rosalie Gamble Hawthorne has a lot of clout. Not because of her tireless activities in support of the arts—such as founding the Looney Ladies Gallery, which never reopened after its COVID-19 shutdown in 2020—but because she's a Gamble. There's no older money in town. Her father is Josiah Gamble, president of Gamble Bank & Trust. And the stately Gamble Building, wherein my office is located, was named after her great-great-grandfather, who funded it. So, her nomination of Williams for the alumni award was significant. I accessed the Cody memory banks for what I knew of him.

Nobody in our little town of Erin, Ohio, is especially impressed by—or even thinks much about—the fact that a local citizen's name is famous from New York to Paris. One such name was Parker Williams, at least among devotees of comics and graphic novels (the latter being longer, among other differences). Williams was well known as the artist-writer for Paragon Comics who created Red Falcon, among other superheroes—and supervillains to match. In fact, I gathered he was one of the major attractions at an upcoming comic con that was a big deal for a community our size. I'd visited his studio some time back during a murder investigation with Sebastian McCabe.[1] And I knew that Williams was to speak to the group of aspiring mystery writers called the Poisoned Pens at our monthly meeting in eleven days. No warning bells in any of that.

"Why is it not good?" I asked Richards.

"Personally, I don't think the three marriages and the womanizing during and in between makes him a great candidate for being honored by a Catholic university." *Nobody's perfect, Kelly.* "There would be blowback about Williams getting the Chandler just for that. But I'm even more concerned that he's been charged with plagiarism."

If Mac were here, he'd raise an eyebrow.

After a dramatic pause, Richards went on:

"His character Red Falcon has a very popular new foe called Queen Bee. She's a crime lord who kills her emerging rivals using insect venom, hence the name. She has an army of worker bees to do her bidding. And in her secret identity she's a professor of entomology with a lavish lifestyle to fund."

"Isn't that a little hokey?"

"Don't argue with success, Jeff. The next Red Falcon movie is going to be built around the character, with Winsome in the part." I would have whistled if I knew how to whistle. I don't need to tell you that Winsome Lerouge is as much a one-name celebrity as Oprah or Winona. She's been A-list since that James Bond movie *Dragonfly*, which also starred Heather O'Toole. "And now a freelance writer claims

---

[1] See "Dead on the 4th of July" in *Murderers' Row* (MX Publishing, 2020.)

that he essentially created Queen Bee with a different name in a character outline and a story he sent to Williams on spec three years ago. He's making a lot of noise about it."

"And this came to your attention how?"

Richards straightened up in her chair and studied the blank notebook in her hand so that she didn't have to look at me. "I read TMZ, the celebrity news site," she confessed. "It's one of my guilty pleasures. They carried the story a few weeks back. It stuck in my mind because I happened to see Miranda Blackwood in the first Red Falcon movie."

"And maybe happened to read a Queen Bee comic book or two?"

"Graphic novels," she corrected. "But I'm no expert."

"Of course not."

"Mac knows far more about the genre than I do. So does Sister Polly."

As SBU's Lorenzo Smythe Professor of English and head of our minuscule popular culture program, Sebastian McCabe is on top of all that stuff. But this was the second week in January and my brother-in-law was communing with his fellow Sherlock Holmes wizards in New York at the annual Baker Street Irregulars Weekend. I don't know everything that goes on there, and probably don't want to, but I'm sure they don't sit in their hotel rooms. It's a social weekend, and Mac is a very social creature. And right now, he needed the break. He'd been brooding around for months, gloomier than a London fog because he didn't exactly shine in his last outing as an amateur sleuth.[2] He got it right in the end when

---

[2] See *The English Garden Murders* (MX Publishing, 2022).

no one else did, but that didn't seem to soothe his bruised ego.

Fortunately, with Mac and my sister Kate in the Big Apple, I had a good backup for the intel I wanted. Sister Mary Margaret Malone, aka Sister Polly (but I call her Triple M), has been improving her mind with the output of DC, Marvel, and Paragon Comics since she was in military intelligence before entering the convent. She's also a big fan of mysteries and belongs to the science fiction book club which, like the Poisoned Pens, meets monthly at Mo's Mysteries & Marvels bookstore. I made a mental note to drop into her office at Campus Ministries when I had a chance. More importantly, I told Popcorn to remind me. I could just call Triple M, of course, but I like to get around campus and I hadn't been to that end of it in too long.

Since it was only a couple of weeks into the winter term and approaching the Martin Luther King holiday, things were blessedly quiet on the job that afternoon. We didn't get a single media call. So, Popcorn and I parallel played in our respective offices for most of the afternoon, conferring occasionally as necessary. Approaching her 60th birthday that year and still fighting the scale despite her daily jog, my dyed-blonde associate is the ying to my yang. Some people would say she's the brains of the outfit, and I'm one of them. As a small department in a small university, the two of us handle most of SBU's communication needs with occasional help from consultants, freelancers, and work-study students who intern with us. But that could change. I have some ideas.

About four o'clock, having dealt with the more pressing items on my to-do list, I wandered onto the TMZ website for the first time. It was like a supermarket tabloid without the restraint. I put "Queen Bee" into the search engine. (Mac says the magnifying glass on those things is a "signifier" of Sherlock Holmes.) Up came three stories, all with photos and headlines below. The first, from just a few weeks earlier, was headlined **SUPER ROW OVER SUPERVILLAIN** and it began:

> Freelance writer Gavin Frost-Pierson is rocking fans of graphic novel superstar Parker Williams with allegations that Williams's Queen Bee supervillain is a rip-off of a similar character he created called The Stinger.
>
> "She was my idea, and I was stupid to send Williams a sketch and an outline of a story," Frost-Pierson said. "I thought we could work on it together."
>
> He concedes that the story, called "Stung," was never used.
>
> "It's the character that's valuable," he said, "not what she's called or the storyline. The real money is in the movies, and they butcher the material anyway."
>
> "That's a crock," Williams told TMZ. "I never heard of this guy."

If Frost-Pierson had any proof, the story didn't say so. Nor did later stories, which featured a lot of sniping back and forth and fans weighing in on a subject about which they couldn't possibly know the truth.

I'd just finished reading the third story when Popcorn popped her head into my office. "Why don't you go see Sister Polly before she leaves for the day?"

She didn't have to say it twice.

TRIPLE M, A five-foot-six bundle of energy with blue eyes and short black hair parted in the middle, hangs her metaphorical hat (she doesn't wear a veil) in a small office overflowing with books of theology, spirituality, and science fiction. Students drop by there to talk about their lives and woes and maybe their loves for all I know. The inspirational posters on the walls were now joined by one advertising the Tri-State Comic Expo.

"Shouldn't that be 'Graphic Novel' Expo?" I asked.

"Don't be sarcastic, Jeff."

Who, me?

The Expo had my attention because it was to be held on SBU property, although not on campus and not as a university event. More on that later. The advertising poster promised the appearance of a number of superhero-related actors from films, TV shows, and cartoons (Miranda Blackwood, Winsome, Scarlett Featherstone, Tamsin Crowley, and Llewellyn Chase), as well as comic book artists besides Williams (Howard Landsman, Red O'Connor, Jake Davis).

"So, tell me about Red Falcon," I said, settling into a seat. "All I know is that she was played in the movie by the gorgeous Miranda Blackwood, who married Parker Williams, although we never see her in Erin." I'd also seen drawings of the character in Williams's studio during that one visit, and thought his latest wife seemed a good fit for the role.

"She's awesome! The character, I mean."

"What's her superpower?"

"She doesn't have one—that's what makes her so awesome," Triple M enthused. "She fights crime with brains and brawn. As Kimberly Shaw, she's an Olympic gold med-alist who works in a crime lab. But she's frustrated at the pace of justice, so she takes matters into her own hands by putting on the red costume and searching the city—Capitol City, that is—at night for crimes in progress."

"Why is she called Red Falcon, other than the fact that she wears red tights and red cape?"

She shrugged. "Why not?"

"Good point."

My eyes roamed between the poster on the wall and books on the shelves. Triple M must have noticed the trajectory because she said:

"Comics are highly theological, you know. They're all about good triumphing over evil, as in Red Falcon winning out over Queen Bee and the other bad guys and girls. And it's almost a truism that the Superman backstory is really the Exodus story."

"Exodus? As in the Bible?"

Triple M nodded. "Obviously, the infant Kal-El, who becomes Superman, being sent off the dying planet Krypton in a rocket ship is like Moses being put in a basket and floated down the Nile to safety." *Obviously!* "That's just one famous religious parallel. There are whole books about the theology of comics—sin and salvation in bright colors."

"I'll take your word for it. On the matter of sin, what about Parker Williams and 'thou shalt not steal'? Kelly Richards says he's been accused of plagiarizing the Queen Bee character."

"Yeah, that's been a hot topic on social media. There was even an implied death threat that got somebody banned."

"A death threat against Williams?!"

"No, against his accuser. And I said 'implied.' Something like 'watch your back, Frost-Pierson.' Parker Williams is really popular, although some women think his women are a little too womanly, if you know what I mean." She waggled her eyebrows. Having seen drawings of Red Falcon and Queen Bee, both of which had curves to rival not only Wonder Woman but even my uber-shapely spouse, I knew what she meant.

"Do you think the plagiarism accusation against him is true?"

Triple M looked thoughtful. "I have no idea, but if so, it wouldn't be the first time something like that happened. A man named Bill Finger was the co-creator of Batman, but he didn't get full credit for decades—not until after he was dead."

On that not-so-cheerful note, I stood up. "Well, Williams was only one of several nominees for the Chandler Alumni Award. With any luck I won't have to deal with any pushback from Mr. Gavin Frost-Pierson."

"I KNEW A GUY named Gavin Pierson when I was in college at OU," Lynda mused over her Manhattan that evening at the Cody manse, our Arts & Crafts bungalow on Campion Lane. Ohio University (not to be confused with the Ohio State University) is two hours northeast of Erin, and ten times bigger than SBU. My beloved wrinkled her brows in thought, by no means distracting from her lovely oval face or her cutely crooked nose. Our three kids were off playing at the moment, and I'd been giving a war report on my day. Lynda's is divided between the kids and her home office. She's become a regular Lynda Teal Cody Inc., what with her saga novels and her popular true crime podcast based on Mac's cases. "Gavin was a little older than me, but also a journalism major. We sort of, um, dated for a while."

Sort of?

"Define 'a while.'"

"Oh, a couple of years. I'm sure it's not the same guy, darling."

A couple of years! Why had this never come up before? But on the other hand, why would I be surprised? Lynda was a bright and beautiful woman in her twenties when we met. She had to have had boyfriends before me. Lots of them! In fact, I wonder how many?

While all this was rocketing through my head, Lynda was sitting next to me on the love seat. Suddenly, she was sitting much closer, and I knew why it's called a love seat. Her curly, honey-blonde hair was soon in disarray.

"Whether this Frost-Pierson is the same guy or not," I said later—quite a bit later—"I'm glad he's not in Erin. With my luck, he'd probably wind up murdered."

A month later, he was in Erin.

Chapter Two
Red Bull

IT WASN'T A coincidence that I saw Parker Williams (aka Mr. Miranda Blackwood) less than two weeks after that visit from Kelly Richards. *Au contraire*, as Mac would probably say, I decided to attend the meeting of the Poisoned Pens on that fourth Monday in January precisely because Williams would be holding forth there on detectives in comics and graphic novels.

Since I gave up writing private eye novels in favor of these true crime accounts, I seldom join the aspiring mystery fictioneers of which I am a charter member. But Richards's warning about Williams had given me the urge to see that popular culture celebrity again. Besides, the assurance of my artist sister Kate that Mo's Mysteries & Marvels wouldn't be big enough for Williams and his ego made me think it might be fun. It was no chore to get Mac to join me. He drove us there in his ginormous (big enough to hold his sizable girth) 1959 Chevy convertible, fire engine red with tail fins.

"What we now call graphic novels are a fascinating art form in their own right," he assured me as he piloted the land yacht. "Most often we think of them in terms of the superhero genre, and yet, all forms of literature have been found between their covers—mysteries and horror quite notably. And incidentally, have you ever seen the wonderfully illustrated 'Love Song of J. Alfred Prufrock' online?'"

"I'm waiting for the movie."

Ignoring my acerbity, Mac went on to say something about graphic novels becoming movies and television shows, while movies and television shows can become graphic novels—"sometimes *too* graphic, old boy."

And so forth.

Nobody ever said that Sebastian McCabe can't lay on the verbiage. And all this in a drive of less than ten minutes! He didn't even bother to light a cigar, sparing me the near-asphyxiation I often suffer in his beast of a car.

Mac is, of course, guilty of committing numerous mystery novels featuring a magician named Damon Devlin, none of which has a nodding acquaintance with plausibility. Thus, he is no stranger to the Poisoned Pens.

But except for him, Parker Williams was the first published writer to speak to the group since Dunbar Yates, author of the semi-hardboiled Hector Gumm & Beauregard mysteries (Beauregard being a Bluetick Coonhound). That was back when the Pens met at the old Pages Gone By bookstore, before a murder investigation led to the arrest of one of the Poisoned Penmen.[3] Other than that, the membership of the group was pretty much the same under the able leadership of my pal Maureen Russert, the "Mo" of Mo's Mysteries & Marvels, with the exception of a couple of additions. (Mac is an allegedly silent partner in the store, although the idea of him ever being silent is worthy of a laughing-face emoji.)

---

[3] See *Bookmarked for Murder* (MX Publishing, 2015).

Mo, a sweet soul with a pleasant face and dark bangs, was talking as Mac and I entered the former fire station on Water Street somewhat late.

". . . my good fortune to strike up a conversation with Parker one day here at the store about detectives and super-heroes," she was saying. "It turns out that they have more in common than you might think. So, he agreed to come here and talk to us a little about that."

Mo and I went out together a couple of times when we were both single—which, for the record, is nothing re-motely like dating for two years.

As she went on with the intro, heavy on accolades, I studied Parker Williams. Although his hair was Andy Warhol-white, he was only in his mid-forties, with hazel eyes behind thick, black glasses that reminded me of binoculars. At the rate he was chugging Red Bull, I feared that just watching him was going to keep me awake that night. Also, he looked like he needed a cigarette. And I know that look from Lynda's nicotine days. By the time I focused on what he was saying, he was well into lecture mode on the subject of the evening.

"People forget that early superheroes like Batman, the Elongated Man, and J'onn J'onzz,[4] also called the Martian Manhunter, were detectives first and foremost," Williams as-serted. "Does anybody know the name of the comic book where Batman first appeared?"

Mac didn't even have to stroke his sizable beard over that one. "*Detective Comics*," he rumbled.

"Right." Williams appeared nettled at somebody an-swering correctly. He quickly filled in the details, maybe to beat Mac to it: "*Detective Comics*. That was in 1939, issue

---

[4] This is the correct spelling of that venerable character's name—*S. McC.*

number twenty-seven, in a story called 'The Case of the Chemical Syndicate.' So even the title indicates that it's a mystery. By the way, the character was called The Batman then, just like the new movie that's coming out. And when Bob Kane first created him, The Batman was more like The Shadow, a mysterious presence solving mysteries and striking fear into the hearts of superstitious criminals."

And I thought: *What about Bill Finger, Kane's co-creator who died poor and alone?* By this time I'd done enough research to know that although Kane had the basic idea and the name for the character, the writer Finger was largely responsible for suggesting the iconic appearance of the cowled Dark Knight.

"Oh, I loved The Shadow," Mary Lou Springfield volunteered. A retired school librarian whose efforts at mystery-writing put the "hard" in "hardboiled," she's no spring chicken. But she's also not old enough to have caught the classic radio show or the pulp magazines when they first appeared back in the early 1930s. She must have picked up the fandom from her parents. As always, Mary Lou sat next to long-time beau Roscoe Feldman, who has been working on a locked-room mystery with echoes of both John Dickson Carr and Mary Higgins Clark for longer than I've been married.

Williams refueled from the can of Red Bull and went on. "The 50th anniversary issue of *Detective Comics*, from March 1987, is a pure detective story by Mike W. Barr called 'The Doomsday Book.' It has Batman and the Elongated Man pursuing a case related to one faced by Sherlock Holmes a century earlier. And in the end, Batman meets an aged Holmes who is still alive thanks to a special formula of royal jelly and the atmosphere in Tibet, where he now lives in hidden retirement."

"Ah, yes, the earlier Holmes case forms a separate chapter based on Dr. Watson's tantalizing reference to 'the repulsive story of the red leech,' which he never recorded," Mac filled us in. "It turns out that the leech was to be Professor Moriarty's means of assassinating Queen Victoria."

"I have that issue," announced Harvey Duncan, who looks like Santa Claus in a beret. Not for nothing had he been Erin's favorite Father Christmas until he began spending his winters in Florida. He'd come back to Erin early this year for some family reason. So far as I know he hadn't actually written anything since joining the Poisoned Pens several years back, but there was always hope.

Williams looked as if he wanted to tell Duncan "I'll alert the media," like the butler in the movie *Arthur*. And Mac appeared to be fighting hard not to say, "I have two copies, one of them framed."

"So, I guess the anniversary story was kind of a callback to the Caped Crusader's origins as a supersleuth," put in Ashley Crutcher, an upbeat brunette in her mid-thirties. "And at the same time an homage to Holmes." As paralegal to Erica Slade, Erin's top defense attorney, Ashley sees crime close up in her day job. Even worse, one horrible time murder hit not just close to home but in her home.[5] And yet, she remains a cheerful reader and writer of mysteries, plowing forward with her widowed life and slimmed down from the days when I first knew her. Something in Williams's gray eyes told me that he was measuring her for a tight-fitting superhero costume and not finding her wanting.

---

[5] See "Dogs Don't Make Mistakes" in *Rogues Gallery* (MX Publishing, 2014).

"Well, yes, that's all true," he condescended. "But my point is that many of the great comic superheroes are detectives in the sense that they have to solve some sort of mystery or mysteries as part of defeating their villains. It's just more obvious in some storylines than in others. For instance, in 1989 there was a Batman vs. Jack the Ripper one-shot called *Gotham by Gaslight* featuring a 19th-century Bruce Wayne operating in an alternative universe. And there was a great 13-issue limited series in the mid-1990s called *Batman: The Long Halloween*, later printed as a graphic novel. That one is about a murder-a-month serial killer, with each killing tied to that month's holiday. In each issue, or chapter, Batman meets up with one of his traditional villains—the Riddler, the Joker, Poison Ivy, etc. But enough about Batman. I guess I'm here because my own Red Falcon stories are mainly mysteries, with a lot of action thrown in."

"Action built around a protagonist who is something of a vigilante," Mac tossed in. "Which is much in the tradition of Batman, if you do not mind my saying so."

Williams looked like he minded a lot as he finished off his can of Red Bull with a vengeance and then retorted: "You might as well say in the tradition of Zorro or any other character who ever donned a costume and a *nom de guerre*. They all operate outside the law to a degree, to do what the law cannot. Kimberly Shaw became Red Falcon because she saw so many criminals going free for lack of evidence, chain of custody issues, or pure bungling. I am proud to say that many women regard her as a role model."

"What good is that when it's a role that none of them can possibly live up to?" riposted Jessica Ballantine, a lean but muscular woman with dark hair shorter than mine and a pixie-cute face innocent of any makeup. In her early twenties, she somehow looked even younger in her untucked red plaid shirt and white jeans. "Real women are without power."

Mac raised an eyebrow, as he is wont to do. I could tell without looking that all eyes were on Williams, who looked as if he'd been slapped. And in a sense, he had been, verbally.

"Excuse me?" Williams said. "I'm proud to say that all of my comics are filled with powerful women." *Like the villainous and possibly plagiarized Queen Bee!*

"The whole Paragon Comics universe is filled with big-boobed women whose lives are nothing like the lives of real women," Ballantine shot back. Now they were in a staring contest, and Ballantine was winning. She's a volunteer firefighter as well as a personal trainer at the Nouveau Shape gym, where Mac once broke a leg trying to get healthy. I've been a little scared of her ever since Mo told me she wrote a story about a woman who kept her husband prisoner in the basement. But I've not heard that she was ever married.

Williams forced a chuckle. "If you are saying that my work is not about ordinary people leading ordinary lives, I plead guilty to writing within my genre. The best graphic novels have serious themes but take place in a world not our own. If fantasy disturbs you, stay away from social media."

"Fantasy? As in the adolescent male fantasy of Red Falcon, you mean?"

The situation rapidly spinning out of control, Mo Russert stepped in before Williams could answer.

"So, Parker," she said, "how did you come up with the name Red Falcon?"

Ballantine shot Mo a venomous look from a pair of ocean-blue eyes. Apparently welcoming the change of topic, the artist-writer responded quickly with: "I cribbed it from two Dashiell Hammett novels."

Plagiarism again!

"*Red Harvest* and *The Maltese Falcon*," Harvey Duncan wheezed. I was impressed, not figuring Santa for a fan of the hard-boiled school.

Parker nodded. "That's right. I've always been a fan of Hammett's writing, including his Secret Agent X-9 comic strip that started in the mid-'30s. My plotlines might owe a lot to the Golden Age greats like Agatha Christie and Ellery Queen, but every superhero carries a bit of Sam Spade, the Continental Op, and X-9 in terms of being quick with fists. And Red Falcon is no exception."

This is no time for me to throw in a Sebastian McCabe-style lecture on the Golden Age of detective fiction, that time roughly between the two world wars of the twentieth century. Just say "too clever by half" and you've got it, although Mac wouldn't agree. He'd throw around words like "ingenious" and "mind-boggling," with side-lectures on locked-room murders and least likely suspects. But you get the picture.

"There is one trope with which graphic novels are re-plete, and Golden Age mysteries are not, and it all started with Sherlock Holmes," Mac pontificated.

"The supervillain," Roscoe Feldman supplied before Mac could, causing Mac to raise an eyebrow. I was surprised, too. If you walk into a room and no one's there, it's probably Roscoe. He's the most nondescript person I've ever known, medium in everything except intelligence—and endurance, I guess. I don't just mean dating Mary Lou. He also taught English at Archbishop Bernardin High School for decades and was said to be good at it. "Professor Moriarty was the first master criminal in fiction," he added.

"Right you are!" Mac bellowed. "Of course, Holmes compared Moriarty to a spider, whereas Red Falcon's Queen Bee takes her name from an insect of the apiary variety rather than an arachnid. It occurs to me that Holmes himself was a beekeeper. Is there a connection, Mr. Williams?"

"None. That's just a coincidence."

"And I suppose it's just a coincidence," Ballantine jabbed, venomously, "that the character of Queen Bee is almost exactly like a female supervillain created by another writer and sent to you on spec."

Williams shot up out of his seat, but not too far because he wasn't a tall man. "That's a crock! If that loser—what'shisname—if he were here, I'd deck him. I'm tired of dealing with that delusional claim of his."

Ballantine didn't respond in words, letting a smirk do the talking for her.

"Would you draw a Red Falcon for me?" Ashley Crutcher asked. She held out an artist's sketchbook to Williams. He grabbed it and went to work. "A pleasure," he muttered.

Chapter Three
In the Red

FAST FORWARD eighteen days.

"Young people are starting their careers awash in far more red ink than previous generations," Associated Press reporter Morris Kindle informed me over the phone, as if I didn't know about the student debt crisis. "I talked to a newly minted veterinarian who said she owes $400,000. She only has to pay a percentage of her salary, but that means that after twenty years she'll owe $700,000 because of compound interest on the loans."

This sort of horror story was familiar to me, what with such debt clouding the futures of not just doctors, lawyers, and M.B.A.'s, but liberal arts graduates as well. There was a pandemic-related moratorium on federal student loan repayments at the time, but that only affected a relatively small amount of the total debt outstanding. Without getting into the weeds on the specific numbers, which include lots of variables, the limit on federal student loans doesn't put a dent in tuition at a lot of schools. So, most debt overall came from private sources and isn't covered by the moratorium.

"Here at St. Benignus University, we are laser-focused on keeping costs low so that students don't have to borrow so much to begin with," I apprised Morrie. I'd been through this the previous month with *Higher Ed Insider*. "I'm sure you remember that SBU actually cut tuition when the campus reopened after the pandemic shutdown. And we managed to keep the increase to just three percent this year, well below the inflation rate. We're the best private college value in the tri-state, Morrie, maybe even the Midwest."

And so forth. I was on my game. I had a good story to tell, and I knew how to tell it.

That was the first call I took on that second Friday in February 2022. Up to then, I'd been working on press releases and bantering with Popcorn about Valentine's Day on the upcoming Monday—*St.* Valentine's Day, Mac insisted on calling it, giving the martyr his due.

"So, what romantic gesture do you think Oscar has in mind for you?" I'd asked to get the ball rolling. "Flowers, candy, wine, a basketball game?"

My tenth wedding anniversary was three months away, and Popcorn had been dating our beloved police chief Oscar Hummel since shortly after the nuptials. But I don't think they'll tie their own proverbial knot as long as Oscar's mom is still alive, and I expect that to be quite a while. She was 91 when she breezed through the first COVID variant.

My indispensable number two gave me a coy look as she handed me a cup of defanged java. "Do you really want the details, Boss?"

"Heavens, no!"

"What are you doing for Lynda?"

"I bought her a silver and turquoise brooch made by a local crafter."

"Her birthstone!"

"Right. You know how much she's into that kind of thing. And I wanted to take her out to dinner at Ricoletti's on

Monday, but she insisted on making us a big Italian lunch at home that day instead. Should be very romantic, assuming I make it through the weekend."

"Are you that stressed about the Super Bowl?"

Lynda and I were hosting a party at our house on Sunday, with Oscar and Popcorn among the guests.

"No, it's that Tri-State Comic Expo thing." Popcorn being Popcorn, I didn't have to explain that I was referring to the three-day gathering of comic and graphic novel fans mingling with the artists, writers, artist-writers, and actors named on the poster in Triple M's office. The con was being held at our recently opened SBU Towne Center in downtown Erin, but it was sponsored by the Graphic Images comic book store with some financial help from the Sussex County Convention & Visitors Bureau. (That the president of the bureau is Ralph Pendergast, who hated SBU's popular culture department when he was our provost, is irony to savor, and I savored it.)

"Doesn't that start tonight?" Popcorn said.

"Yes, but that's mostly for the diehards who will probably go all three days. Lynda and Triple M"—my name for Sister Polly amuses Popcorn—"aren't dragging me there until tomorrow, thank heavens."

"What, you don't like superheroes?"

"Sure I do, but I'm not wild about superfans who argue over stuff like whether Stan Lee or Jack Kirby was more important, and I'm guessing this rodeo will be jam-packed with them."

My reference to the iconic Marvel legends made me think of Parker Williams, who was one of the artist-writers to be featured at the Expo. I sent up a prayer of thanksgiving that the accused plagiarist wasn't honored with the Everett P.

Chandler Alumni Career Achievement Award for which he was nominated. The honor went to the founder of a non-profit urban farm that employs people with intellectual and developmental disabilities. Bullet dodged!

"I'd like to go just to see some of the stars, but Oscar isn't interested." Popcorn sighed. "Winsome will be there!"

Almost a decade after her *Dragonfly* debut, Winsome Lerouge was still a hot property as well as a single-name personality. And that upcoming Queen Bee role had her lovely face on a lot of checkout-counter movie magazines. Erin may seem like a strange place to hold an event that could attract such an A-lister, but it's not far from the Cincinnati/Northern Kentucky International Airport and within a short drive of major Midwest cities. And being a small town keeps the cost of conferences and expositions low compared to a metropolis like, say, Chicago.

"If you really want to go, I'll trade places with you," I said hopefully. "That would have the added advantage of sparing me the extortionate hourly rate that Lilly Inouye charges these days for babysitting the Cody offspring."

She shook her head. "We're taking Oscar's mother out to a late brunch at the Mimosa on Saturday for her 93rd birthday, since you insisted on knowing. Just the start of a wild Valentine's Day weekend."

I thought of any number of responses to that but, being an ace communicator, I sipped my decaf instead.

"Is Mac going to the Expo?" Popcorn asked.

We'd looked at each other and broke out laughing. Before I could comment on the impossibility of the big guy not going, my cell phone had rung with the first call of the day.

"Hi, Jeff. Morris Kindle, Associated Press." After almost two decades of doing this dance together, he still has to wave his AP cred every time he calls me, which is fairly often.

"Hi, Morrie."

"I'm working on a story about the student debt crisis. Young people are starting their careers awash in far more red ink than previous generations . . ."

Popcorn blew me a kiss as she smiled her way out of my office.

Chapter Four
Red Anger

"DID YOU HAVE TO wear that, T.J.?" Kate asked, pointing at my *Sarcasm Is My Superpower* sweatshirt. I didn't dignify this big-sister quibble with a response.

She, Mac, and Triple M were attired as civilians (though Mac was sans his usual bowtie), while Lynda's curve-clinging getup as Captain Marvel was—marvelous!

The Tri-State Comic Expo was already hopping when our quintet descended on SBU Towne Center at about 9:30 A.M. Saturday. A sea of fans, a good proportion of them in character for cosplay and a costume contest, thronged the aisles. Some of the characters, such as Spider-Man and Batman, I recognized; some of them, including one with huge red wings, I didn't. Two years after the start of the pandemic maybe a quarter of them wore protective masks, a few of which worked quite well with their costumes.

Two rows of artists sitting at tables drawing their signature artwork to sell were outnumbered about three to one by vendors hawking comic books, collectibles, and costume weapons in another part of the room. I didn't see any Hollywood stars that I recognized, their appearances being limited to panel discussions and a couple of hours of signing their names. But I learned later that some voice actors associated with popular animated programs were on the floor all day,

such as Llewellyn Chase, who voiced the villainous Nightmare, and Tamsin Crowley, who was Captain Zero. There
were also some individuals sitting around looking bored; I
learned later that they were less well-known writers. Presumably pencillers, inkers, colorists, and letterers—though vital
to the production of comics, as I learned later from Kate—
were even more anonymous.

Confabs of this sort weren't the primary reason
Grant Kingsley ("GK"), president of SBU, pushed to create
the Towne Center at the former site of the long-defunct
Kozinn Department Store on Vine Street, between Broadway
and Main. He established it as an innovation hub for budding
student entrepreneurs. But the large, open first floor makes it
eminently rentable for conferences of several thousand people coming and going. The Tri-State Comic Expo was the
first such—and would turn out to be an unforgettable one.

We'd forked over $35 per person at the door for a
Saturday-only ticket, and I was grateful not to be roped into
a bigger expenditure of time and money. Of the five of us, I
was the least interested in being there. Lynda likes superhero
movies, Triple M reads comics, Kate is an artist, and Mac—

"My knowledge of comics and graphic novels is cur-
sory," he informed us, "but I have taken an interest in the
work of Parker Williams since we encountered him in that
Fourth of July murder."

"Boxes and boxes worth of interest," Kate explained.
"As in, frequent trips to Graphic Images, that comic book
store. He's catching up on what he's missed over the past
twenty years."

"Closer to fifteen, my dear. And he created Red Falcon only a scant decade ago."

The hall was overstocked with Red Falcons, by the way—in all shapes and sizes, and both sexes. Genderbending wasn't rare among those in costume. I noted a female Flash and a Wonder Man, for example. Although, I have to say I prefer the originals. Especially Wonder Woman. Speaking of which—

"There is an interesting connection between Sherlock Holmes and the Amazon Princess," Mac said, oblivious as ever to the fact that his idea of interesting is not always shared by the mere mortals around him. "Wonder Woman's creator, William Moulton Marston, attended the 1936 dinner of the Baker Street Irregulars. He was a psychologist who also invented an early lie detector."

"Rebecca is a big fan of Gal Gadot's Wonder Woman movies," Kate commented. "She'll be here later." The "she" being Rebecca, not Gal. The oldest of the McCabe brood at almost 23, Rebecca had survived a change in majors from arts education to graphic design. She was now on track to receive a Bachelor of Fine Arts degree from the Department of Art & Design in SBU's Rev. Joseph F. Pirelli School of Arts and Humanities. An independent sort, she lives in the apartment above the McCabe garage where I was domiciled for many years before getting married to Lynda.

As we ambled our way through the crowd, watching artists at work and gawking at costumes, I heard the geeks around us engaging in spirited debates about who was the best Robin in the comic books ("Dick Grayson, of course!"), whether Marvel or DC or the much smaller Paragon put out the best graphic novels, and how awful it was that a school board in east Tennessee removed something called *Maus* from the eighth-grade curriculum the previous month.

"Isn't that Parker Williams?" Lynda asked.

Yes, it was he, with a long line of fans standing in line to have comics signed or order up one of the drawings-on-demand that he was dashing off for $75 a pop. I'd been told how this works: He would take commissions in the morning and deliver them by the end of the day.

"Shalimar!" That was Triple M hailing a thirty-something black woman with long and curly strawberry blond hair, dressed in nondescript jeans and a denim jacket.

"Sister Polly!" It came out as a whoop. The two women hugged, which made third wheels out of the rest of us until Triple M broke the embrace to introduce her friend as Shalimar Burton, "social media influencer on TikTok, Instagram, YouTube, and Twitter."

"And what do you influence your public to do?" Mac wanted to know.

"Be a superbabe, every one of them!" Burton gave a smile that could have lit up New York City in the middle of a power outage. She opened her jacket to show off a T-shirt emblazoned with the word and a nicely done caricature of herself pumping iron while dressed in a small amount of swimwear. "Every day I send off style tips and inspirational messages that remind my followers that a woman of any size or color can slay dragons, move mountains, reach their goals, and be free."

That word "free" suddenly caused the Cody memory banks to kick in. I now recalled a press release that our intern, Riley St. Simon, put out about Shalimar Burton: She was freed from prison as a result of an Ohio Innocence Project effort by SBU's criminal justice studies program. And, of all people, Mini Cooper—once a prime candidate for a life of crime herself—was the driving force in the successful campaign to right the wrong. The details eluded me. But I was sure that Riley was following Burton on all forms of social media; that's in her wheelhouse.

"How admirable!" Mac proclaimed. "It does not take much imagination to see the connection between your social media enterprise and the theme of this Expo."

"You got that right! I always tell my followers, 'You're your own Doctor Doom and your own kryptonite. Nobody can defeat you but *you* as long as—'"

"Idea thief! Plagiarist!" It would be an exaggeration to say that the high-decibel accusation, hurled by an angry man in a Cleveland Guardians baseball cap about fifty feet away from us, caused the room to go still. But he had our attention. The guy, with a face almost as crimson as the cap he was wearing, was shouting at a stunned Parker Williams. "You stole the character you call Queen Bee from me and the whole comic world knows it!"

"I wouldn't put it past him," Shalimar Burton said, not softly. Before Mac or I had a chance to seek details on that, Lynda exclaimed, "OMG! That's Gavin Pierson, my old b— Um, a guy I knew in college."

"He kind of looks like you, Jeff," Kate said.

Which was ridiculous. This Pierson or Frost-Pierson was two or three inches shorter than my six-one. And his hair that I could see, what wasn't covered by the baseball cap, was sandy, not red. Also, he wore round glasses, of which I have no need while not reading. But before I could deny any similarity of appearance, Lynda—Captain Marvel—squeezed my hand and assured me: "You're much more handsome, darling." *Who am I to disagree?*

Oblivious to our sideshow, the confrontation between Williams and his accuser continued until—

"Knock it off," a short woman in the crowd with Princess Leia hair told Frost-Pierson. "This con has standards of behavior, and you're violating them."

"I'll go, but I won't go quietly," Frost-Pierson said, looking from Williams to the artist's defender. "You can expect to see me again at the panel." He stalked off.

"I can understand why Mr. Williams's fans are unhappy with that fellow," Mac said.

"Yeah, I wouldn't want to be his life insurance company," I quipped.

"Well, Williams is certainly a great artist-writer," Kate said. "If you don't believe me, just ask him."

To be fair, this negative impression of the man's self-regard was based on Kate's rather limited experience of Parker Williams. He spoke once as a guest lecturer for her class on "The Art of the Graphic Novel," which she offers every few years as an adjunct professor in Mac's popular culture department. On the other hand, my two encounters with Williams gave me no reason to think she misread him.

As Frost-Pierson moved on, so did we. We saw a lot of familiar people in the hall: Batman, Green Arrow, Captain America, Nightmare, the Hulk, Aquaman (and several Aquawomen), various X-Men, Captain Zero, Superman, and their super-ilk. But also, not a few SBU students who hailed Mac by name; Aaron Patch, our next-door neighbor; Gene Pfannensteil, head librarian of the Lee J. Bennish Memorial Library on campus; Mary Lou Springfield and Roscoe Feldman, of the Poisoned Pens; the bombastic Lafcadio Figg, Mac's old frenemy; and, most surprisingly to me, Amy Quong, executive vice president of Gamble Bank.

"The bank takes a strong interest in all activities that bring vitality to our community," she explained in the cool manner of the ace businesswoman that she is. No superhero costume for Amy Quong; she wore a pink dress with a flower pinned to her bosom. But was that flower a scarlet pimpernel? Perhaps a nod to literature's first superhero with an alternative identity?

Panels started at 11 A.M. and were scheduled to continue until a costume contest at 5 P.M. The rundown, as detailed in the program we were handed on entering, was:

11 AM
Spotlight on Red O'Connor and Jake Davis
Silver Age Memories

12:30 PM
Blowing Wind concert

2 PM
Spotlight on Scarlett Featherstone
What's Next for Soldier

3 PM
Spotlight on Winsome Lerouge
Queen Bee Without Sting

4 PM
Spotlight on Parker Williams
A Platinum Age for Graphic Novels

5 PM
Tri-State Comic Expo Costume Contest

6 PM
Spotlight on Miranda Blackwood
Red Falcon Flies Again

We dropped in on the first panel, held in a partitioned-off area on the ground floor, about five minutes late because Mac got into a stimulating (to him) conversation with an artist-writer named Frank Cho about drawing Sherlock Holmes. The large room was maybe half full, although people drifted in and out. Two guys in their mid-seventies to early eighties were on stage gassing about what it was like to work for outfits like DC and Marvel in their youth. Said youth was during what's called the "Silver Age of Comic Books," which Mac tells me was from 1956 to about 1970. They each held a microphone.

"The companies got the silver; we didn't," said the one identified by his nameplate as Red O'Connor, although his full head of shaggy hair was now as much gray as red. He had bags under his watery blue eyes and a pot belly beneath his suspenders. His line about silver drew a laugh, but O'Connor didn't look like he was kidding.

"Yeah, but think of all that fame we got," bantered back Jake Davis, who reminded me of an aged Stan Laurel. Like the previous laugh line, this one apparently carried a bit of truth. Both artists were inkers, and Davis went on to say that inkers first began to get credits on comic books during the Silver Age. Kate explained later that in traditional comic book publishing, an inker—also called a finisher or embellisher—outlined and finalized a drawing created by a penciller. A letterer then inked the text and a colorist added color. Got all that? The complexity of the process gave me new respect for the craft.

"If the Silver Age was followed by the Bronze Age, what age are we in now?" O'Connor wondered.

"Plastic," rasped Davis, probably a heavy smoker.

And so forth.

We stayed all the way through what was to me a torturous Q&A session ("What was Steve Ditko really like?"). Then we grabbed lunch from food vendors on the second floor and listened to Blowing Wind, which turned out to be a duo of twin sisters with an amazing ability to produce superhero movie theme-songs out of an oboe and a flute.

Back on the ground floor, the room in which the panels were conducted was filling up, but the audience profile was about the same as for the Red & Jake Show. Looking around, I saw comic book aficionados dressed in costumes from She-Hulk to Thor and sporting various shades of hair from pink (a younger-than-me woman not dressed for cosplay) to green (the Joker). Intern Riley St. Simon's magenta pigtails would have fit right in, but she wasn't there.

Scarlett Featherstone, star of the first panel after the concert, should have used her acting skills to pretend to be interested in the questions lobbed her way by a chunky interlocutor with wavy hair and a thick mustache. At age 28, Featherstone had only last year made her film debut in the eponymous role of Soldier, a VA nurse by day and camouflage-wearing vigilante by night. This was another Paragon Comics character created by Parker Williams. The actress was shorter than she looked in film clips I had seen, no taller than five-six, but wore a red dress that made it apparent she was every bit as well-built off camera. She had brown eyes and a lot of brunette hair that she was careful not to let obscure her lovely face.

"I've never actually read a comic book," she said at one point in response to a question about how her PTSD-suffering on-screen character differed from the comic book version. "My parents would never allow it."

Her questioner barely skipped a beat at that shocking admission. He continued gamely on with asking Featherstone questions about the process of making the film, what she thought of the other actors in it ("Hugh Laurie was amazing!"), and the timing for the sequel.

"I'm ready whenever Paramount is," she responded to the latter, showing the most enthusiasm of the day.

Winsome, fresh off the filming of *Queen Bee* in the title role, was either a better actress or telling the truth when she said during the next panel that she'd wanted to play the part ever since learning the flick was in development.

"Who wouldn't want to play such a great villain?" she enthused in her veddy British accent.

That was her answer to one of several softballs pitched by Al Daponte, the large, loud, and balding owner of the sponsoring Graphic Images store. She fielded all of them deftly. ("Well, a film is different from a graphic novel, so there are a few changes. But I don't think Red Falcon fans— or Queen Bee fans, for that matter—will be disappointed.")

With her golden hair in a chignon, the beautiful Winsome looked every bit the part of the bee-sotted crime queen, although more casually dressed in slacks and a blouse.

The Q&A part of the panel got a little more pointed when a young woman in a Supergirl T-shirt asked:

"Is it true that you and Miranda Blackwood barely speak to each other?"

Winsome chuckled. "Don't believe everything you read while you're in line at the grocery store, my dear."

But you didn't say "no," Winsome.

Supergirl pressed on: "Word is that you got quite friendly with her husband, Parker Williams, during the making of *Queen Bee*."

Out of the corner of my eye, I saw Mac raise an eyebrow.

"I think I met the man once before today." Winsome sounded exasperated. "There's just nothing to that stupid rumor. I think it got started in the *National Enquirer*, which I wouldn't use to line my birdcage—if I had one."

Daponte thanked the young Supergirl (insincerely) and the questioning moved on to less controversial matters. ("What is Martin Freeman really like?")

When the hour for that panel was up, the five of us stayed in the room but took a seventh-inning stretch.

"What do you think?" Lynda asked the group at large. "Are Williams and Winsome stepping out on Miranda Blackwood?"

"I have no data," Mac said. "It is a capital mistake to theorize before one has data."

"Maybe we shouldn't talk about that; there is a sin called detraction," Triple M said. Which means damaging somebody's reputation, even if what you say is true. I looked that up once. "I can't help wondering what Parker Williams would say, though. His panel is up next."

But five minutes after the scheduled four o'clock start of that session, Williams still hadn't taken the seat vacated by Winsome. His inquisitor, a young woman dressed as Nick Fury, started to squirm. At ten minutes after, with the room quite noisy with jabber, Al Daponte's employee Bobby Lumpkin hobbled to the front of the room on crutches. Bobby is in his mid-forties, pudgy, with an unkempt beard and wire-rimmed glasses. "I'm sorry Parker isn't here yet," he said. "He must have had some sort of unavoidable delay. Thank you for your patience."

Seconds later, Kate's phone rang. "It's Rebecca," she said, swiping her finger to answer the call. Although the speaker wasn't on, I could hear my niece's distraught voice on the other end. Words tumbled over each other in a rush:

"Mom! It's horrible! I'm upstairs. The elevator opened and I saw the body and it was all bloody and I knew right away who it was." *Gavin Frost-Pierson*, I thought instantly. But I thought wrong. "Parker Williams. Somebody killed Parker Williams."

Chapter Five
Blood Red

WE ALL RAN up the escalator, Kate in the lead. Well, the corpulent Sebastian McCabe can't exactly run, but he did his best while calling 911 at the same time.

The second floor of SBU Towne Center has office space, but also a series of open areas designed to be flexibly adapted by entrepreneurial types. On this second day of the Tri-State Comic Expo, it hosted a random selection of vendors—spillover from the floor below. We found the bank of two elevators, which opened into a hallway facing restrooms and not visible from the rest of the floor. Rebecca, wearing a classic red-white-and-blue Wonder Woman costume, sat there holding her knees. She bounded up and into her mother's arms when we entered the hallway.

"Oh, Mom! He was—"

And then came the tears pouring out of eyes that were already red.

"You don't have to talk," Kate told her.

Mac said nothing, just stood looking more helpless and directionless than I had ever seen him in our nearly thirty years of friendship.

One of the elevator doors was open, affording an unpleasant view of what had once been Parker Williams. Sightless hazel eyes stared out of heavy black glasses and his pale blue knit shirt was stained with blood around the heart area. My niece, showing a presence of mind that blew me away, had pushed the red button to stop the elevator before she called her mother.

While Mac, Lynda, and Triple M attempted the impossible task of comforting mother and daughter, I walked around a corner and made two necessary phone calls: First to my boss, Lesley Saylor-Mackie, who wears two chapeaux as both executive vice president and provost of St. Benignus University. Then to Cal Daley, head of SBU's Department of Public Safety. This was a death on university property, and they needed to be notified.

"How dreadful for Rebecca!" exclaimed the usually serene Saylor-Mackie, an elegant, gray-haired personage who had once been mayor of Erin. "Thank you for calling, Jeff. I assume you will stay there and be of whatever help you can? Good. Please convey my concern to Mac and Kate, as well as to Rebecca. Keep me posted as events unfold. I'll inform GK and Dr. Nelan." *Better you than me.* Our president wasn't going to be happy about this particular kind of publicity for his pet project, of which Susan Nelan, professor of entrepreneurship studies in the Gulliver Mackie School of Business, was the director.

"And I'll call Cal," I said.

Daley, whose Department of Public Safety includes St. Benignus University Police (SBUP) under the direction of long-time chief Ed Decker, would know about the murder soon in any case, but I wanted him to know even sooner. His initial reaction to my news is best left unrecorded. Then he said: "This is going to be a jurisdictional mess." He didn't actually say "mess." What he meant was, the campus cops—sworn, weapon-carrying officers under Ohio law—and

Oscar's troops would have to work together on this one. But given the personalities involved, Daley was over-worrying.

"I'm sure Banfield and Gibbons can work it out," I said with some irony. The two super-competent assistant chiefs have been known to keep company on a very friendly basis outside of working hours, being mutually smitten with each other.

By the time I disconnected from Daley, I was already mentally crafting an official SBU comment along the lines of "horrific event . . . details not yet available . . . fully cooperating with the Erin Police Department . . . prayers are with Mr. Williams's family . . ." That was my job—and concentrating on it kept me from thinking too much about what Rebecca was going through now and maybe for some time to come. She was my first niece and I'd held her in my arms just hours after she was born on a hot June day.

When I got back to the elevator from making the calls, there was a new player on stage: Oscar Hummel occupied the hallway along with Mac, our spouses, and Triple M. The poor man looked like he needed a cigarette. He usually does, although Popcorn doesn't even want him to vape. With too many pounds and too little hair, the chief of Erin's Finest is pushing his sixth decade hard. He'd been dragged away from his mother's birthday luncheon with Popcorn at the restaurant of the nearby Winfield Hotel, judging by the seldom-worn suit beneath his topcoat and the ancient gray homburg covering his balding noggin.

"Take your time," he was telling Rebecca. "I don't want you to feel like you have to—"

"It's okay," she said. "There's not much to tell. I wasn't interested in the Parker Williams panel, so I came up here to look around instead. That didn't take long. There's a lot of fake weapons for sale, which I didn't want to buy, and a dealer offering to buy old comic books, which I don't have to sell. So, I was going to go downstairs and just hang around and kill time until the costume contest. I pushed the button for the elevator, it came, the doors opened, and"—a catch in her voice—"there he was. I knew right away *who* he was, and I was pretty sure he was dead."

"You knew him?" Oscar asked.

Rebecca shook her head. "No, but somebody pointed him out to me once. Maybe Jessica Ballantine. I'm not sure."

It didn't occur to me to wonder how Rebecca knew Ballantine, the antagonist at that memorable Poisoned Pens meeting. There were a dozen ways, especially since the two young women weren't that far apart in age.

"Okay. You knew he was Williams and you thought he was dead. You stopped the elevator, right?"

"Yeah."

"Why?"

She shrugged. "I don't know. Instinct, I guess. It just seemed the thing to do."

Oscar turned to Mac.

"You're awfully quiet for a change."

Mac grimaced. "I believe it would be inappropriate for me to question my—our—own daughter."

What I think he meant was, he didn't have the heart for it. But it had to be done, and the Chief was doing it in a reasonably delicate way.

Oscar hmphed. "'Inappropriate' never stopped you before. Besides, it's not like she's a suspect."

Lt. Col. L. Jack Gibbons, clad in civilian chinos and a leather jacket, pushed past me just then to interrupt this love fest with a report to the Chief: "Lehmann and Mentzel are securing the scene to make sure that nobody leaves."

Oscar nodded. "Good."

"The killer might well have left the building already," Mac pointed out.

"Thanks," Oscar told him acidly, "but I hope you can do better than that to help us wrap this up. This is exactly your kind of case."

"I am no longer certain there is 'my kind of case'," Mac volleyed back. "Three people died because I didn't trust my instincts enough to see a clue that was right in front of me in that English garden business."

He meant it, but Oscar persisted.

"Don't give me that. This is screwy, Mac, and you specialize in screwy. It's almost like a whatchamacallit—a locked-room mystery."

Mac lifted an eyebrow. "How so?"

"This wasn't a shooting from yards away. I've seen enough gunshot wounds to know that without moving the body until the coroner gets here. Williams was probably stabbed, meaning the killer had to have been in the elevator with him. So how did said killer leave without Rebecca seeing him when the elevator doors opened to show a body inside?"

The McCabe mind made short work of that, after mulling it over for half a minute.

"I suggest that what happened was this: The killer came today armed with a knife and looking for an opportunity. That occasion arose when he—or she—was waiting on the main floor to board the elevator, the doors of which opened to reveal Parker Williams alone. Realizing that no one else was in the immediate hallway vicinity—because a good portion of the participants were in the panel session and the rest in the main hall—the killer quickly boarded the elevator, stabbed Mr. Williams out of sight of anyone who might chance to enter the hallway, then pressed the second-floor button and quickly exited before the doors closed. That concealed the body and removed it from the first floor while giving the murderer ample time to discreetly leave the building before the body was discovered and the alarm could take place. Q.E.D.[6] It was a combination of preparation meeting opportunity, also known as luck—good luck for the killer, bad luck for the victim."

"Oh," Oscar said, chastened. "You're saying the murder was premeditated, but not the time and exact place. Yeah, I guess that makes sense in real life, even though I wouldn't buy it for a minute in one of your mystery novels. Good thing this isn't a book."

But it will be.

Lynda bit her lip in thought. "Why didn't the killer throw the body out on the first floor and ride the elevator up here to establish an alibi far removed from the scene of the murder?"

"An excellent question!" Mac said, getting sucked in more deeply by the moment, despite his declared reluctance. "He or she probably acted instinctively to get rid of the body, rather than getting away from the body. However, that action also had an advantage over your scenario, Lynda: This way, no one could have chanced to see the killer leaving an elevator that just came from the floor where the murder happened."

---

[6] The abbreviation of *Quod erat demonstrandum*, which is a fancy way of saying in Latin, "there, I proved it."

"That would be a pretty remote connection," Triple M objected. "There are a ton of people down there. You're thinking like a mystery writer."

"To that I plead guilty."

"Which begs a question," Kate said. "If you're planning to kill someone, why do it with all these people around?"

"Precisely because there *are* all these people around, my dear," Mac said. "The Tri-State Comic Expo constitutes a rather large haystack to sift, does it not, Oscar?"

The Chief grunted.

"And although it was possible to pay in advance," Mac sailed on, "that was not required. Cash was accepted at the door as well as credit cards. The killer could have left without any indication that he or she was ever here."

"At least we stopped the bleeding," Oscar said. "Nobody left after my men got here. We'll run background checks on them all for connections to Williams."

"I'm sure a lot are from out of town," Triple M said.

"That's going to be a pain in the ass. Sorry, Sister." *As if she'd never heard the word before. Cripes, Oscar, you know the woman was in military intelligence before she joined the Sisters!* "I can tell them, 'Don't leave town,' like I did in the Speakeasy case,[7] but they can tell me where to shove it." *Back to that part of the anatomy again.*

I sensed a certain dissatisfaction on Oscar's part.

"We should start by interviewing the visitors," Gibbons said. He rations words like they're gasoline at current prices, but what little he says is always worth listening to. Mac hopped on his train of thought with:

---

[7] See *No Ghosts Need Apply*, (MX Publishing, 2021).

"I suggest you begin with an individual named Gavin Frost-Pierson—"

"Gavin!" That was from Lynda.

"—who was known to have an animus for the victim. He is the classic obvious suspect—almost too good to be true, in fact."

Mac explained the background.

"What does he look like?" Gibbons asked. Armed with a description, he phoned Officer Mentzel and told him to find the dead man's adversary. Then Mentzel talked. "Wait a minute," Gibbons told him. And then to Oscar: "Mentzel says a man named Daponte is demanding to see you."

"Who the hell—"

"The owner of Graphic Images, sponsor of this shindig," I explained.

Oscar sighed. "Send him up. He may know something useful."

"Send him up," Gibbons said into the phone. "Oh? Send her up, too."

"Who else?" Oscar demanded.

"Assistant Chief Banfield."

"The more the merrier, I suppose." Oscar sounded glum.

Gibbons referring to his main (and only) squeeze Banfield so formally caused Triple M to emit a snicker worthy of the Army veteran that she is. Aurelia Banfield is military, too—National Guard, with Afghanistan service that cost her a leg. She arrived on the second elevator, along with Daponte. Sporting a weekend look, Banfield was dressed in civies with her long brown hair hanging free. She carried a backpack over her shoulder as if it were a purse. As number two in the

University police, she hadn't been part of the routine security detail that the Expo sponsors paid for.

"Chief Decker sent me," was her opening line. "I'm here to liaise." Everybody in that hallway knew that she liaises with L. Jack Gibbons on a regular basis (see Triple M's snicker), but they also knew that SBU's end of the case was in good hands with Banfield.

"What the hell happened here?" Daponte demanded loudly. He had his white shirt sleeves rolled up to show a tattoo of the iconic Superman logo. It occurred to me that I wouldn't want to get in a bar fight with him. In fact, I wouldn't even want to be in a bar with him.

"Murder," Gibbons said.

"Probably by knife, judging by appearances," Oscar added.

Daponte swore. Oscar glared him into silence.

"Of course, there is the highly improbable prospect that Parker Williams committed suicide and that someone removed the weapon," Mac said.

"Why would anybody do that, Seb?" Banfield asked. Nobody else calls my brother-in-law by that jaunty nickname. We wouldn't dare.

"Even my fertile imagination fails to conceive of a reason, Aurelia; that is why I called the scenario highly improbable. However, under the famous dictum of Sherlock Holmes, only the impossible can be eliminated."[8]

"Somebody should tell his wife," Daponte said.

"Is she here?" Oscar asked.

---

[8] "When you have eliminated the impossible, whatever remains, *however improbable*, must be the truth."—*S. McC.*

"Yeah—Miranda Blackwood, the actress. She's scheduled to be on a panel at six o'clock, which will have to be canceled. What a shitshow! I haven't seen her, so she may still be in her room at the Harridan Hotel."

"I'll have Officer Bertsch find Ms. Blackwood," Gibbons said.

I knew Bertsch; she was a 2021 graduate of SBU in criminal justice studies.

"Good. Have them meet us—where?" Oscar looked at me. "We need to set up someplace other than the crime scene to talk to suspects."

"Sue Nelan won't mind if we use her office in the northwest corner of this floor," I said. I sent a quick text to keep her in the loop as I said this. I've known the director of the SBU Towne Center for years in her professorial capacity. She responded to my news seconds later with a frown face emoji.

"Okay, then that's where we'll go." Oscar nodded toward Gibbons, who picked up his cell to call Bertsch. "Arly and the EMTs will be here soon. Not to mention the press. I think non-essential personnel need to skedaddle pronto."

"Must I stay?" Mac asked.

"Yeah."

"Am I essential?" I wondered.

"Not to me," Oscar said, "but you can stay because you're Mac's Watson."

"I am *not* his—"

"What about me?" Daponte asked.

"Go, but don't leave the building in case we need you. Rebecca,"—Oscar turned to her—"you can go with your mom now, but come down to the station on Monday to make a formal statement. And take care of yourself."

This was a kinder, gentler Oscar Hummel than the one who first came to Erin more than a decade ago, probably due to Popcorn's influence.

Triple M and Lynda cleared out along with Kate and Rebecca. Just as the four of them got on the down escalator, Sussex County coroner Dr. Arlene Eppensteiner and the EMTs emerged from the second elevator.

"Murder by kryptonite?" she said by way of greeting.

After almost six years on the job as an elected official, Arly Eppensteiner is slightly more cynical but just as energetic—five-foot-one of hard-working public servant with frizzy dark hair. Ohio law doesn't require the coroner to be on the scene of suspicious deaths, but she does so whenever she can. She must keep a white lab coat and vitrile gloves in her car.

"We were thinking maybe a knife to the heart," Oscar said dryly.

A few minutes later the coroner offered her opinion, based only on visual examination, that "a thin blade, possibly a stiletto" had entered the victim's heart, "although, of course, I can't even semi-officially say that was the cause of death until the autopsy."

"Knives and swords are all over this place today," Banfield observed. "Maybe it was a sword." She seemed to find the notion exciting.

"They're all fake," Daponte said. "Carrying real weapons is a serious violation of the Expo policy."

Add that to the killer's offenses.

"Have the troops check all such blades," Oscar told Gibbons, as if he needed to. "Maybe one is real." Then he turned back to Daponte: "How many people are here?"

"I can't give you the count right this minute, but we expect five thousand over the three days that started yesterday. That's only about a fifth of what Cincinnati gets for its comic book expo, but it's huge for this microplex."

Barely registering "microplex" as a Ralph Pendergast term for our small city and county if I ever heard one, I watched with a strange feeling of disconnect as the EMTs put the body of a man I'd met onto a stretcher for transportation to the morgue. Then I noticed items near the body.

I pointed. "What's that?"

One of the EMTs picked up a pen and a small notebook, or maybe a sketchbook, 3½ inches by 5½ inches with a spiral on top. There were just two words scrawled in it:

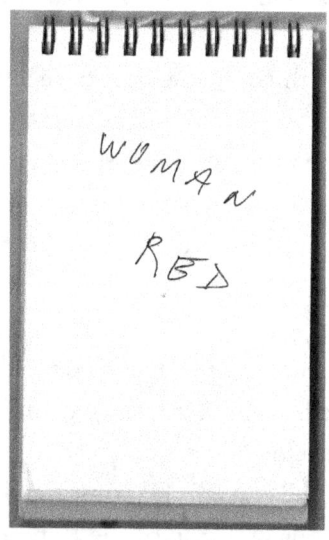

Chapter Six
Seeing Red

"MR. WILLIAMS TRIED TO Identify his killer!" Mac said.

"Well, he should have tried harder," Oscar said. "Hell's bells, what's 'red' supposed to mean?"

"Clearly, the victim did not know or did not recognize his assailant, and therefore in his dying moments wrote the only thing that he knew about her," Mac said.

"Like what, she had a bad sunburn?" Sarcasm isn't Oscar's superpower.

"Maybe she wore a red protective mask," Banfield offered. "Or a red superhero costume."

"Not much help," Gibbons said monosyllabically. "Even Ms. McCabe's Wonder Woman costume is mostly red."

"As are the other three hundred Wonder Woman costumes here," I exaggerated. "And a red protective mask could be whipped off in seconds."

Oscar looked as thoughtful as one can while wearing a homburg. "Maybe Williams was going to write 'redhead' before he ran out of life."

"If so, that would be a good clue," Mac said. "Although approximately ten percent of the Irish population and six percent of the Scottish have red hair, the worldwide figure is only one to three percent." *Everybody knows that, Mac.* "That would make for a rather small universe of suspects."

Too small, I thought, given that Kate and I have deep red hair and Rebecca is a ginger.

"Two percent of five thousand is a hundred people, many of them in costumes," Eppensteiner noted as she pushed the "down" button of the second elevator car. The murder car was sealed off with crime scene tape for photographing and fingerprint dusting. "So, good luck with that." *Killjoy.* "I'll call you with the autopsy results, Chief. It won't be today."

"Sure," Oscar told the closed elevator door.

By "results," the coroner meant the bottom-line oral version of the results; the written autopsy report that nobody without an M.D. degree could understand would take another 12–14 weeks. And it could have been worse. A lot of counties in Ohio outsource coroner services. Montgomery County alone handles all the autopsies for 35 of the state's 88 counties.

"Five thousand attendees was my estimate over the course of the Expo, not how many were in the building an hour ago," Daponte pointed out.

"Getting back to redheads," I said, "red happens to be a very popular color for women to dye their hair these days."

"How do you know that?" Banfield wondered.

"Lynda mentioned it a couple of weeks ago. Her hairdresser, Myrtle White, told her." *And I'm not sure the information was worth the $3 price hike the last time Lynda had her hair styled. Although it did look great!*

"In reality," Mac said, "the word 'red' could mean so many things as to be almost meaningless—shoes, slacks, blouse, skirt, dress, scarf, jewelry, lipstick, fingernails—"

"A flower!" I put in.

Mac raised an eyebrow.

"Amy Quong is wearing a red flower, although that's probably just a red herring." *Sorry; I couldn't resist.*

"Indeed. As I was about to say, at this early stage it seems most likely that the killer was someone cosplaying as a female superhero, or perhaps a female version of a male one."

"Well, the place is crawling with Red Falcons," came the inappropriately cheerful voice of our good friend Johanna "Tall" Rawls as she entered the hallway. News of the murder must have traveled like the Flash to bring the award-winning reporter for the *Erin Observer & News-Ledger* out on her off day. Maybe Johanna received a tip from Quong. The banker had served on the board of our local newspaper ever since Serena Mason—who has more money than Scrooge McDuck—bought it from Grier Newspaper Group. But a quick text from Lynda, her mentor and journalistic role model, was the most likely source. I never asked.

"Ah, the press," Oscar said. "Just what I need to make my day even better."

The leggy blonde smiled but otherwise ignored the unoriginal jibe as she pulled out her notebook. "What happened?"

Oscar gave it to her straight: "Someone stabbed Parker Williams shortly before he was scheduled to appear on a panel. Miss Rebecca McCabe found the body in that elevator." He nodded toward it.

"Poor Rebecca!"

"At this point, that's all we know."

"Not quite," Johanna objected. "Mac was just saying something about the killer being dressed up."

"That's just speculation. I'm sure you're only interested in the facts." That was neither irony nor sarcasm. Trained in journalism by Lynda, my favorite reporter is, well, a reporter—not an opinion writer flying under false colors. Maybe that's why she still works for a small-town paper. The Chief looked at Mac as if to say, "*Should I give her the whole enchilada or not?*"

"There seems little reason to play our cards close to the vest in this situation," Mac opined. "Whatever Mr. Williams's message means, that will not be changed by the murderer reading about it in Johanna's story."

Oscar looked doubtful, but he told Tall Rawls:

"We found a notebook near the body in which the victim wrote the words 'woman' and 'red.' That may well have been written in his dying moments as an attempt to say something about his killer."

"I'll say! I mean, what else could it be, Chief?"

"Well, for instance, it could be a note he wrote to himself before he was attacked, say an idea for a comic book he was working on." I was impressed by Oscar's spitballing. "It's really too early to say, Johanna. The body is barely cold. But don't quote me on that—it would be insensitive."

Oscar, insensitive?

Cop and reporter verbally jousted for a few more minutes, then the latter went off to write her story.

"At least we know that if what Williams wrote *does* describe the killer, it was a woman," Banfield said.

"Or someone dressed as a woman," Mac countered. "There is that in abundance at this expo. Or perhaps there were two killers—a woman and someone associated with the color red."

"But you yourself used a female pronoun for the killer right after you saw the note!" I objected.

"Upon reflection, that was premature."

This is where I usually get a headache and Oscar starts to sputter. But before either could happen, Gibbons suggested we leave the crime scene and move to the location I'd suggested for conducting interviews.

Sue Nelan's office is spacious and uncluttered, with a large picture window overlooking Vine Street. Oscar commandeered her impressive walnut desk and got comfortable, removing his hat and overcoat. Mac and I grabbed seats, but Gibbons and Banfield chose to stand.

Officer Mentzel arrived almost immediately with Gavin Frost-Pierson, looking hostile and still wearing his Cleveland Guardians baseball cap—red with the team's name in blue.

"What's this all about?" he demanded.

"You didn't know?" Oscar asked in a dangerously neutral tone. "I'm Chief Oscar Hummel of the Erin Police Department. There's been a murder."

Mentzel wouldn't have told him about Williams's demise when he brought him in, but I thought the SBU Towne Center would be buzzing with the news. Apparently not, however.

"Murder? Who?" If Frost-Pierson's expression of surprise was acting, he was good at it.

"Parker Williams."

The eyes behind his round glasses opened wide. "Holy shit!"

"Did you kill him?"

"What the— Hell, no!"

"Surely you do not pretend to be unhappy at his demise?" Mac said.

"Gobsmacked, that's what I am. I hated the asshole, but—murdered? Holy shit!"

"And you had both motive and opportunity," Oscar informed him. "That brings us to means, as in knife. Will you submit to a search?"

"I'm not saying or doing anything until I call my lawyer."

"So call him."

"Her." He whipped out his cell and pushed a number on his "recents" list. He made no attempt to lower his voice when his party answered. "Felicity? You won't believe this. Somebody murdered Williams and the cops are looking at me!" We couldn't hear her response. He went on: "The Tri-State Comic Expo—that's where it happened. We're on the second floor, two left turns off the only elevator that's working. How soon can you be here? Good. See you then." He hung up. "She'll be here in ten or fifteen minutes."

Mac arched an eyebrow. "Your attorney is local?"

Frost-Pierson nodded. "She's been handling my legal claims against Williams. Felicity Snow."

The name wasn't familiar to me, and neither Mac nor Oscar commented on it.

Frost-Pierson put his phone back in his pocket and crossed his arms. The body language was clear, but I made a bet with myself that I could get him to talk.

"Didn't you used to be just plain Gavin Pierson?" I asked.

"Ancient history," he said. "I changed it when I got married. Why should my wife be the only one to hyphenate her name? And how the hell did you know?"

"*My* wife told me." I was having fun dragging this out.

"Who's your wife?"

"Lynda Teal . . . Cody."

"Lynda?! Really?"

"She sends her regards," I lied politely.

"Who are you, then?"

"Lynda's husband."

"This is Jeff Cody and that's Professor Sebastian McCabe, both of St. Benignus University," Oscar said in a formal tone. "They are occasional consultants to the Erin Police Department. I asked them to be here. And that's my assistant chief, Colonel L. Jack Gibbons, and Assistant Chief Aurelia Banfield of the St. Benignus University Police. We're on SBU property. Now that we're all introduced, it's your turn to talk."

"Okay." Frost-Pierson looked at me. "How's Lynda? I'd love to see her. I bet she has a bunch of kids."

"Three, including twins."

"Really? Wow! Did she become—"

Oscar interrupted with, "That's not what I meant by talking. I was hoping you could answer our questions."

"Not until my lawyer gets here."

That made for a long fifteen minutes before an attractive black-haired, blue-eyed woman swept into the office. She was medium-sized, built like a runner, and probably under the age of 35.

"I'm Felicity Snow, Mr. Frost-Pierson's counsel," she announced briskly. "Are you all right, Gavin?"

"Fine, now that you're here. But still pissed."

Snow presented her business card all around, each of us doing likewise to show we weren't intimidated. "I've heard of you, of course," she told Mac. Her face and build seemed vaguely familiar to me in turn, which I put down to probably having seen her around town.

Mac bowed. "Only good things, I hope."

She smiled slightly and turned to Oscar without answering. "I would like a few minutes to confer with my client in private, please."

After some back and forth, Oscar agreed to let Frost-Pierson and Snow have the office alone.

"What do you think they're talking about?" I asked as we waited it out in the hallway.

"She's asking him if he did it," Banfield said.

"Does it matter to her?" I asked.

"Only in terms of defense strategy," Mac averred.

"Why might he have done it, by the way?" Banfield asked. "I'm a little late to the party, remember."

Not waiting for Mac to put it into polysyllables, I jumped in to brief her on the Queen Bee controversy and the shouted confrontation between the two men earlier that day. It helped to pass the time until Snow called us back into the room.

"Mr. Frost-Pierson is innocent of any wrongdoing, much less murder, and he will be happy to answer any and all of your questions with complete candor," she announced. "He will also submit to a search."

"I didn't kill Williams," her client said, just to be clear, "and I'm lucky his crazy fans didn't kill me. I was the subject of a death threat on Facebook—'watch your back.'"

"The animus of those Parker Williams devotees is understandable," Mac said, "given the vigor of your allegations against the object of their affections. You were quite forceful in your denunciation of him this morning. I would even describe you as angry—seeing red, in fact."

"Damned right I was, and I was going to give him even more hell at his panel." The look on Snow's face told me he hadn't run this brilliant plan past her. "Williams stole my character, The Stinger, and renamed her Queen Bee."

"An injustice which, as Mr. McCabe indicated, we are fighting vigorously in hopes of an equitable settlement that would involve royalties for the use of Mr. Frost-Pierson's character in future comics, graphic novels, and movies," Snow said. "My client had every reason to desire a long and productive life for the deceased."

"Just out of curiosity," I said, "do you have any proof for the plagiarism claim? I haven't read about any in the media coverage."

Snow thought about that before deciding to answer: "We have a copy of the sketch and story outline that Mr. Frost-Pierson sent to Parker Williams. Although Williams denied receiving the material, Kit Frost-Pierson—my client's wife—can testify that she recalls him drawing it years ago. And we are prepared to identify seven ways in which the character of Queen Bee draws on The Stinger, most notably her profession as a professor and her signature penchant for killing her underworld rivals with bee venom."

"Just like a real queen bee," Gibbons said. As if on cue, his phone rang. After a quick check to see who was calling, he answered "Gibbons" on his way out the door.

Snow turned to Oscar. "Do you have any questions for my client, Chief?"

"Yeah." Oscar turned to him. "Where were you when Williams was killed?"

"When was that?" Frost-Pierson asked.

"About an hour ago."

"I was up here on this floor."

"Not downstairs impatiently waiting for Mr. Williams's panel to begin?" Mac asked.

"I lost track of the time while I was talking to a guy who buys comic books published before 1971. I'm thinking of selling some of mine to raise a little cash. Here, he gave me his card." The name on it was "Rasputin Spargo, Collector," further identified as *"Buyer of Golden and Silver Age Comics and Original Comic Art."*

"Anything else?" Snow asked.

"The search," Oscar said. He stood up and started frisking the suspect.

"What do you do when you're not submitting comic book ideas?" I asked Frost-Pierson.

"I'm a journalist," Lynda's college boyfriend said. "That is, well, that's what I do, but I'm in between jobs right now. The newspaper industry has been closing papers and slashing staffs for years."

This was an understatement, and a source of anguish to Lynda, who calls herself a "recovering journalist." And I knew from a little online research a few weeks earlier that Frost-Pierson had more than his share of pink slips, making his way through a half-dozen or so jobs in journalism and out of it over the past two decades. He and Kit, who was a medical technician, had two young children. Kit's Facebook page showed her to be a pretty blonde (like Lynda!) who looked friendly and posted lots of cat photos.

"Am I correct in believing that you don't live around here?" Oscar asked Frost-Pierson.

"My client is a resident of Akron," his attorney answered. "He's staying in Erin through Sunday night. After that you can reach him through me."

"Thanks for your co-operation," Oscar grunted.

Lawyer and client left.

"Ms. Snow does have a point," Mac said. "Mr. Frost-Pierson had an economic motive for wanting the victim alive, and no motive to kill him other than rage."

"Isn't that enough?" Banfield asked.

"For a heat-of-the-moment assault, certainly it is. However, surely the murder was premeditated, given that the only weapons on sale here are non-lethal and it is unlikely that the murderer would just happen to be carrying a thin blade."

"Copy that, Seb."

"Aren't you ignoring the obvious?" I said, with some heat. "That Cleveland Guardians baseball cap Frost-Pierson was wearing is redder than the ink in the federal budget. And as you said, Mac, there could be two killers—one woman, and one red."

"Alas, Jefferson, although I initially singled out Gavin Frost-Pierson as a person of primary interest, he is one of the last individuals on earth who could have been indicated with the word 'red' in that dying message, if that is what it really was."

"Why?"

"Because we know that as a result of today's confrontation, if not before, Parker Williams certainly knew his *bête noire* by sight. And he even knew that Gavin Frost-Pierson was wearing that particular headgear today. Thus, he would have no reason to indicate Mr. Frost-Pierson as his killer in any way other than by name—certainly not by the color of his cap."

"Oh."

Chapter Seven
Triple Red

OSCAR CHECKED HIS phone and listened to a voicemail. "Always nice to get advice from the citizenry," he grunted after disconnecting. "Ralph Pendergast called to let me know the Convention & Visitors Bureau doesn't want me to shut down the Expo. Not that I could."

I checked my own mobile to find a text from Grant Kingsley: *Update me when appropriate. Counting on Mac to wrap this up fast.* GK, who is possibly Mac's greatest fan next to Mac himself, once compared a university to a small city with its own security force, trash removal, and so forth. If so, he's its hands-on mayor. He came to SBU after successful high-level careers at the Air Force Academy and the Altiora Corp. I wrote back to assure him that Mac was on it, along with the Erin and St. Benignus police.

I'd just about finished with that when Gibbons came back into the room to report, "That was Bertsch calling me from the Harridan. She broke the news to Miranda Blackwood about Williams. Ms. Blackwood appeared to be devastated, according to Bertsch, and asked if we could give her some time before speaking with her. Given that she wasn't on the scene at the time of the murder—so far as we know, anyway—that seemed reasonable, so I said it was okay. By now she's probably on her way to identify the body. Who else do we want to bring in for an interview?"

Oscar looked at Mac. "Any big-brain ideas?"

"Hardly that, Oscar." *McCabe the modest makes a rare appearance!* "It does occur to one, however, that there are several individuals under this roof who have reddish names— Scarlett Featherstone, Winsome Lerouge—'*rouge*' being French for red—and, most obviously of all, the inker Red O'Connor. Of course, with the first two we would not have to posit that 'woman' and 'red' refer to separate individuals."

"But why pick such an obscure way to point to the killer, Seb?" Banfield objected. "He must have known the two actresses by name, just as he did Frost-Pierson."

"Quite so. Hoist with my own petard!" *Whatever a petard is.* "And yet, although it may be without meaning, it is an inescapable fact that Ms. Featherstone and Ms. Lerouge are women whose names are associated with the color red."

"Not as closely as associated as Red O'Connor," I put in.

"He's waiting outside," Gibbons reported.

"I took the liberty of sending Officer Mentzel a text about ten minutes ago suggesting that Chief Hummel might wish to speak to the three individuals we have just been discussing," Mac explained. "Apparently Mr. O'Connor is the first of the trio that he was able to secure."

"Bring him in," Oscar told Gibbons. If the Chief had any thoughts about Mac making so free with instructions to one of his troops, he didn't share them.

I'd seen O'Connor on that "Silver Age Memories" panel, during which I learned that inkers like him never got credits on comic books until the Silver Age, roughly 1956–1970. He was the gray-haired, baggy-eyed, pot-bellied one.

He kind of slunk into the room, like a dog waiting to be hit.

"What's this all about?" His tone was more wary than defiant. Then he answered his own question: "I heard that Parker Williams was murdered."

"You heard right," Oscar said. "Did you know him?"

"Not really. We met here and there. A lot of people thought he was hot stuff. I thought he was pretty good, but no Carmine Infantino, if you know what I mean." *I haven't a clue, Red.*

"He would know you by name then?" Mac asked.

O'Connor stood a little straighter. "He said a few nice things about my work once a few years ago, when we were on a panel together."

"Did you see him today?" Oscar wanted to know.

"Only from a distance. We were both working the tables—you know, drawing on demand. His had a long line. Mine, not so much. Then we both had panels, but I guess he didn't make it to his."

"Just to be clear," Banfield said, "you're saying you never had an issue with Parker Williams?"

"If you mean bad blood between us, hell no! But why the hell does everybody talk about 'issues' these days instead of problems or complaints or whatever? Issues used to be what comics put out every month."

I was starting to like this guy.

"So," Banfield pressed, "when the combined forces of the city and university police"—not exactly the NYPD—"investigate, we won't find out that you two had a big blowup either today or at any time in the past?"

He shook his head. "Double-hell, no."

When Oscar told him that he could leave but should stay in touch and give Gibbons his contact information, O'Connor didn't linger. He went, quietly.

In his wake, the Chief sat back in Sue Nelan's ergonomically designed chair and counted off on his fingers. "Possible motives for O'Connor: Sex, unlikely. Money, only if Williams ripped him off by plagiarizing a character or some such. Revenge is wide open because maybe they really did have issues."

"Plagiarism seems unlikely," I objected. "O'Connor was an inker, not a writer."

"That is no objection," Mac said. "Anyone, in theory, might have a burst of creativity along those lines. For example, Gavin Frost-Pierson, by his own account, has been employed as a journalist."

"Just a different form of fiction." I didn't mean it, but it was fun saying it.

"The only thing really pointing toward O'Connor is that he's called Red," Gibbons pointed out.

"Check his background for anything that rubbed against Williams," Oscar told Gibbons. "There might be something there. He seemed—"

The door opened, and Bobby Lumpkin burst in. Well, more like hobbled. Al Daponte's pudgy employee was on crutches, after all.

"Sorry to interrupt, but this is important."

"It had better be," Oscar fumed. "This is official police business."

"So is what I have. I think you need to take a hard look at Scarlett Featherstone as a suspect." A McCabe eyebrow shot up and Bobby continued: "She has good reason to be totally pissed at Parker. *Soldier* was her first movie, and it made her a name. The expectation was that it would launch a franchise, and she would continue to play the lead. That's like coining money. But if you don't read the comic books that the movie was based on, you might not know that just last month Parker killed off Soldier's secret identity, Kathy Strong, and replaced her with a new Soldier, a transgender woman named Grace Amazing."

"Wouldn't that be like Superman isn't Clark Kent anymore?" Banfield asked. "I mean, it sounds like a really big deal."

"A major shift, to be sure," Mac agreed. "However, it is hardly unprecedented."

"Sure," Lumpkin said. "There was more than one secret identity for Green Lantern, Green Arrow, and Captain Marvel, and there were five Robins."

"Three of whom also adopted the identity of Red Robin!" Mac inserted. "Interesting, that. Is there a Red Robin here today?"

"I don't think so," Lumpkin said, "but I can't be sure."

"Speaking of red-costumed superheroes and multiple secret identities," Mac rolled on, "the history of the Flash's identity is particularly complicated. The Golden Age Flash was Jay Garrick. He was replaced by the Silver Age Flash, Barry Allen. When Barry died to save the world, Kid Flash, Wally West, became the Flash. But then Barry came back to life."

"Is there a point here somewhere?" Gibbons asked, and none too soon.

"Yeah—revenge," Lumpkin said. "If Kathy Strong isn't Soldier, then neither is Scarlett Featherstone. I've met

Featherstone—very entitled and demanding. She can't be happy about losing the role that made her a star, and she's not the type to take that lying down."

"Is that it—what you had to tell us?" Oscar asked.

"Isn't that enough?"

"Thank you for coming forward." *And now get lost* was unspoken but implied.

"You're not buying it?" I asked after Lumpkin departed.

"I wouldn't buy it if he was giving it away," Oscar said.

NEXT UP WAS Winsome Lerouge, dressed in the same blouse and slacks from her panel a few hours earlier. Her golden hair was becoming untucked from the chignon and the makeup on her pretty face could use retouching. In her later thirties, she wasn't exactly reaching her expiration date, but she was a few years older than Scarlett Featherstone and Miranda Blackwood. I stood up and gave her my chair. It's what my father would have done.

"This is just awful," she said, "but I don't know how I can help you. I didn't even know Parker Williams. Why do you want to talk to me?"

Because even though you're British, your last name is French for "the red" and Parker Williams apparently wrote "WOMAN RED" in his notebook as he lay dying.

Putting it that way in my ongoing interior monologue, the absurdity of linking those two factoids hit me. This was like being in a comic book!

"Just routine," Oscar lied to Winsome. "We wanted to talk to some of the out-of-town visitors before you leave Erin. You've already made it clear you don't think you have anything to tell us." He squirmed in his seat. "But I hope you can appreciate that we can't ignore rumors that—"

She rolled her brown eyes, reminding me of Lynda. This was a rerun of the question she'd been asked at her panel session. "It's true that I haven't gotten along with Miranda since *Queen Bee* was announced, but that's for reasons that have nothing to do with the dead man. She made no secret of the fact that she didn't want me to be cast as the Queen, allegedly because I've never played a baddie before. The truth is, Miranda was afraid of being overshadowed by me. And by the way, this is my natural hair color. Miranda dyes hers."

"As for Mr. Williams—" Mac tried.

"I wasn't shagging him."

Well, that's clear.

"Nor had you?"

She smiled with her generous mouth only. "Let me see if I can make this definitive: I wasn't having an affair with him, I never had an affair with him, I never wanted to have an affair with him, and I never thought of having an affair with him."

Even clearer, Miranda, but I'm sensing a certain impatience with this topic.

"Just for the record," Gibbons said, "did you ever meet him?"

She nodded. "I've been thinking about that. This afternoon I wasn't sure, but now remember that he visited Miranda on the set of *Queen Bee* a few times. They are married, you know."

"*Were*," I corrected.

Oscar looked around at the rest of us. "Any other questions?"

"Yeah," Banfield said, "can I have your autograph?" She told us later it was for her mother.

THE VERY FIRST Sherlock Holmes story published is *A Study in Scarlet*. I expected Mac to riff on that when Scarlett Featherstone replaced Winsome in my former chair, but he restrained himself.

I'll skip the part where she expressed shock, dismay, and confusion at being there. I don't mean "there" in an interview room surrounded by cops out of uniform and two guys whose presence must have been obscure to her; I mean "there" in a little Ohio River town she'd never heard of.

"I think I need a new agent," the actress said, soon followed by, "You're not going to do the 'don't leave town' thing to me, are you? I couldn't stand it."

Neither could the town.

"To be honest, I don't have the authority to do that given that you aren't a person of interest," Oscar said. "I don't think we'll have to keep you long. We just have a few routine questions, Ms. Featherstone. Did you know the deceased?"

She shook her head, giving all that brunette hair a workout. "I didn't really *know* know him, if you know what I mean."

"No, I don't know what you mean."

"I knew who he was, and I said hi to him today in that big hall where he was drawing Soldier and Red Falcon sketches. But that was the first and last time I ever saw him."

"The suggestion has been made that you might have been angry with him," Mac said.

"Made by who?"

By a titanic effort of will, Mac didn't say "by whom."

"Never mind that," Oscar said. "How about it? Were you pissed off at Williams?"

"Why would I be mad at a man I'd never met?"

"Because the most recent storyline of the Soldier comic book series involves the death of Kathy Strong and her replacement as Soldier."

"Yeah, I think I heard that. Why would I care?"

"Because it cuts you out of your first starring role," Banfield couldn't help saying.

I was watching her face—it was very watchable—but I couldn't read the look on it. Maybe puzzlement.

"That has nothing to do with the films. Kathy Strong is still Soldier in *Soldier II: Kicking Ass*, and I'm still Kathy Strong. I have a three-movie contract for the part, with an option. So, no, I wasn't angry with Parker Williams. Can I go now?"

Banfield didn't ask for her autograph.

"ACTORS!" OSCAR exploded when she'd departed. "I've had my fill already and we still have a few to go through."

"I should have remembered that there is a venerable film and television tradition of sticking with the more familiar version of a secret identity," Mac confessed. "For example, to the best of my knowledge the only cinematic Flash is the Barry Allen version."

"Now you tell me!"

Then it hit me:

"Wait a minute!" I said. "The Flash is mostly red, with some yellow trimmings, hence the nicknames Scarlet

Speedster and Crimson Crusader. And I saw a woman earlier dressed as the Flash—so she was both a woman and red!"

Oscar brightened up. "That's wacko, of course, but still better than anything else we have."

Chapter Eight
Red Sunday

UNFORTUNATELY, THAT was true—unfortunately because the female Flash turned out to be 17-year-old Naomi Abington. Officer Bertsch established that she spent the entire day at the Expo in close company with her father, Dr. Thomas Abington, who was dressed as Green Arrow. The doctor has a thriving family practice, with a side gig as one of Arly Eppensteiner's part-time assistant coroners.

Mac remembered Naomi as "a very attentive student" in his "Media and Popular Culture" class.

Here's what else happened over the remaining hours of Saturday:

The search for the weapon continued. Amid the dozens or hundreds of knives, daggers, stilettos, and rapiers on cosplayers—why would a superhero need any of those things?—none was real.

Oscar's forces, including some pulled in for overtime, took names of participants for future interviews. There wasn't time to talk to everybody that night. And since nobody (costumed or otherwise) had bloodstains on their clothing or a blade in their possession, it didn't seem necessary or legally possible to detain hundreds of people. "Of course, it is quite likely that the killer departed the Towne Center before the body was found," Mac said, drawing a murderous look from Oscar.

I called GK. There wasn't much loop to keep him in, but I gave him what we had, with an emphasis on Banfield's gung-ho involvement (seeing no need to mention her request for Winsome's autograph). I warned him this was going to be a tough case, and we were still on Day One. He asked me how I thought the Towne Center would come out of this; I assured him that the entrepreneurship hub wouldn't be hurt in the long haul. "But the long haul won't begin until the murder is solved," he said. I couldn't argue with that.

Mac and I had a conversation in the car. Mac: "Lynda and the excitable Mr. Frost-Pierson were more than casual acquaintances, were they not?" Jeff: "Hmph." Mac: "You do not wish to talk about it?" Jeff: "What's to talk about? That was ages ago." Mac: "Chronologically, that is undeniable. And yet, the past has a way of breaking into the present. Perhaps that is what led to today's murder." Jeff: "Hmm."

At 10 P.M., Mac and I departed to our respective homes. Dressed in her favorite kimono—red!—Lynda demanded a full report of everything that happened after she and her Captain Marvel costume (which was fabulous) left the Towne Center. This I delivered. She seemed especially interested in the interviews. ("You can't really think Gavin is a serious suspect. He would have muffed the murder six ways from Sunday, poor dear. I'm surprised he remembered me. No, really, he was pretty scatterbrained.") Then we watched the murder coverage on Cincinnati's TV4 Action News at eleven o'clock with anchor Tammie Tucker. They used the B-roll footage of the Expo from that morning over and over, coupled with stills of Williams and quotes from Oscar.

It was midnight by the time we were ready to go to sleep. "This will make a great podcast when Mac solves it," Lynda enthused as she turned out her light. "Heck, *Midwest*

Murders"—one of her favorite "reality" TV shows—"might even do an episode about it."

On Sunday, the world stopped to watch the Super Bowl, in which the Cincinnati Bengals appeared for the first time in 33 years. The big game even shared page one of the *Observer & News-Ledger* with Johanna Rawls's **MURDER STRIKES COMIC BOOK EXPO**, never mind that Russia seemed poised to invade Ukraine and the Standard & Poor's 500 index was down almost 2 percent in the week just ended. In our part of the world, southern Ohio, Bengals vs. Rams was top-of-mind even for football atheists like me.

Lynda and I spent the hours between Mass and 5 P.M. getting ready for our once-in-three-decades Super Bowl party at Chez Cody, interrupted by a phone call to me from student journalist Cindy Weller. The history and mission of the SBU Towne Center rated only a page 4A sidebar by education reporter Hadley Reams in the *Observer*, but it was the reason Weller was working on a story for *The Spectator*, our twice-weekly campus newspaper.

"Our prayers are with Mr. Williams and his family," I assured Cindy. *Including the two ex-wives.* "St. Benignus University Police are cooperating with the Erin Police Department to make sure that the perpetrator of this awful crime is brought to justice."

"University police—would that mean Assistant Chief Banfield?"

"It would."

"She's a hoot."

And so forth.

A few minutes later, Sue Nelan called and said that Cindy Weller wanted to interview her. No surprise there. I gave Sue a few talking points that meshed with what I'd told Weller ("security has been a focus of SBU Towne Center's operations from day one, which is why we had four officers on site Saturday"), then we exchanged our viewpoints on the Bengals and the Rams.

In between working, I set up a well-stocked bar on the counter between the kitchen and the dining room, which flows nicely into the living room, wherein is located our 60-inch television. Lynda strategically placed snacks all over.

Mac, Kate, Oscar, Popcorn, Triple M, Tall Rawls, and Johanna's vertically challenged boyfriend Seth Miller made up our little party, with the Cody kids (Donata, 6, and Sam and Jake, 4) making appearances. Our guests mostly wore spirit wear. We didn't have any of that, so Lynda donned her chocolate-colored ribbed turtleneck, the cameo necklace from our honeymoon in Rome, black slacks, and taupe Vince Camuto dress booties. I threw on an SBU sweatshirt.

Triple M, the first to arrive after the McCabes, asked how Rebecca was holding up.

"You know how strong she is," Kate said. *Translation: She and I are too much alike to always get along.* "Finding the body was traumatic, but she'll be okay."

Oscar and Popcorn were the last to show, he in a Bengals cap and she in a team-colors orange and black scarf.

"Keep your notebook in your purse," Oscar warned Johanna. "I'm off duty."

The journalist guffawed. "A cop is never off duty, and neither is a reporter. Throw me a bone here. What's the state of the case in the Williams murder?"

She pulled out the forbidden notebook.

"If I had any real news, you'd be the first to know," Oscar told her. "There has been no arrest. We interviewed several parties yesterday, and—"

"Would you characterize them as persons of interest?"

"No. I was about to say that Banfield and Gibbons are working the case today, using the Towne Center as their base of operations, and I'm sure they'll talk to some more individuals. As you know, we let the Expo go forward until its scheduled closing time of noon today."

"Do you think the killer came back to the Expo today?"

"I don't want to speculate about that."

Tall Rawls turned to Mac: "What do you think?"

"I think that dogged police work solves most crimes," the big guy said, "and this one probably will be no exception." He may have even meant that. Or else he was just applying some soap to Oscar. I wasn't sure which.

Back to the Chief: "Have you seen the comments on PublicEye, especially from Bethany Lane?" Johanna asked.

"No."

"He's off-duty," Lynda cracked, Manhattan in hand.

PublicEye is a virtual community for amateur sleuths to offer their conjectures (they do like to speculate) about crimes in the news. It has about 60,000 registered members. The cases of Sebastian McCabe have drawn their attention from time to time, most notably the murder that took place during Mo Russert's honeymoon in Barbados over Valentine's Day weekend exactly five years earlier.[9]

---

[9] See "A Destination Murder" in *Murderers' Row* (MX Publishing, 2020).

"As a member of that online forum, I have followed the comments there with interest," Mac said. "Bethany Lane rather romantically refers to the killer as 'The Woman in Red.' This, of course, calls to mind *The Woman in White, The Woman in Black,* and the Sherlock Holmes film *The Woman in Green.*"

"Of course," I said. "Hey, isn't Bethany Lane the name of a street out in Amish country, near the winery?"

"Maybe," Tall Rawls said. "Anyway, the PublicEye's Bethany Lane pumps hard for the theory that 'the woman in red' was someone wearing a red superhero or supervillain costume. What do you think of that?"

"We can't rule it out," Oscar said.

"That won't help much, Chief," Triple M said, grabbing a handful of corn chips to match the beer in her other hand. She knows him well from her volunteer work as a chaplain for his "guests" at the city jail. "There were tons of costumes at the Expo that were red, at least in part."

"Right," Oscar said, still smarting from his disappointment over the Flash/Naomi Abington fiasco.

"Really?" Seth Miller said. "Costumes?" If you look up "earnest" in the dictionary, you might see Seth's dark hair and bespeckled face. And right now, that visage looked puzzled. Being raised Amish, he would know even less about the world of graphic novel fandom than I do. And apparently Tall Rawls hadn't filled him in. Maybe they had other things to talk about.

"Oh, yeah," Triple M said. She briefly explained the concept of cosplay, informed Seth that the Tri-State Comic Expo swarmed with cosplayers, and expounded on colorful characters in comic books: "DC Comics alone has Red Arrow, Red Devil, Red Hood, Red Star, and Red Tornado,"

Triple M said, "not to mention the Tornado's allies Red Volcano, Red Torpedo, and Red Inferno."

"Don't forget Red Robin," I said, earning a glare from Oscar.

"Noted. And as for villains, there are the members of the Red Lantern Corps in *Green Lantern* and Red Cloud in *Action Comics*."

Mac picked up the lecture:

"The Marvel Universe is graced with the superheroic Red Hulk, Red Raven, and Red Wolf. On the dark side, the hideous face of the Red Skull has served a number of villains since his debut in 1941."

"A very impressive list," Kate said. "But I think you've overlooked the most obvious possibility of all. Maybe the killer wasn't dressed as a DC or Marvel character but as Parker Williams's own most famous creation—Red Falcon."

"Can I have a beer?" Oscar asked.

As I moved to fill the order, Popcorn put her arm around him—a rare PDA on her part. "Forget the case for a few hours, honey. I'm sure Gibbons and Banfield will come up with something. They're hard drivers, just like the Bengals."

Cincinnati was ahead 20 to 16 going into the last five minutes of the game. The Rams won 23–20.

Chapter Nine
Red Roses

DESPITE THAT gut-wrenching defeat for our team, the sun came out the next morning right on schedule. In fact, St. Valentine's Day began rather well.

"How beautiful!" was Lynda's reaction to the silver and turquoise brooch I presented her before waking the kids.

"And here's something for you." She handed me a wrapped package, obviously a book. No, not just a book, a first edition of Mickey Spillane's *Kiss Me, Deadly*, with the dust jacket in pristine condition! I teared up. Spillane, Hammett, Chandler—those guys were my idols during the fruitless years I tried to write hard-boiled detective novels before I found my voice in true crime. "I saw you eyeing it at Mo's, but I knew you were too cheap to buy it," Lynda explained.

"I prefer to say thrifty."

She moved closer. "Kiss me, Deadly."

I obeyed, doing a good job of it. Then we woke up the kids and I whipped up a heart-healthy breakfast of oatmeal with walnuts and raisins, which was well received by my four housemates. (In other words, they ate it.)

The only rough water in this sea of domestic tranquility was the absence of the *Erin Observer and News-Ledger*. The *Wall Street Journal* was on our front lawn when I went out, but not the local paper.

"You can read Johanna's second-day story in the *Online Observer*," Lynda reminded me.

I was already looking it up on my phone. **POLICE SEEK WOMAN IN RED**, blared the headline. The story beneath the Johanna Rawls byline began:

> The Erin Police Department and the St. Benignus University Police spent Sunday looking for clues to a killer that some online amateur sleuths are calling "the woman in red."
>
> Chief Oscar Hummel, of the Erin Police Department, said he "can't rule . . . out" the possibility that the killer of noted comic book artist-writer Parker Williams was dressed as a comic book character at the time of the murder. A small sketchbook containing the scrawled words "WOMAN" and "RED" was found . . .

The whole story was online, but still . . .

"You know I prefer to read a paper newspaper over breakfast," I groused to Lynda. "Besides, you can't do your daily crossword puzzle on a computer screen."

"I can print it out. And besides, I can still work the *WSJ*'s crossword." She bent over and gave me a long, spousely kiss. "Don't let it spoil your day, darling. And please try to get home by noon."

A midday meal at Casa Cody would be a nice treat. I usually eat yogurt and trail mix at my desk, the exceptions most often being SBU business luncheons or noshing over a case with Mac.

"I'll do my best to tear myself away from the press of university business," I promised.

THE WORKDAY BEGAN with a scheduled visit from TV4 Action News for a Valentine's Day feature. Tammie Tucker's co-anchor Brian Rose, playing on his surname, was making a rare excursion beyond the anchor desk—to which he had seemingly been anchored for decades—to conduct an interview with an expert on the psychology of sending roses and chocolates to one's beloved.

Not to be outshone by Rose babbling about roses, I'd lined up psychology professor Valentina Kalashnikov for Valentine's Day. Sometimes you get lucky. Dr. Kalashnikov had taken the time to get her makeup in order, although she still didn't wear as much as Brian Rose. They met in her office. The videographer first recorded her, then Rose's face looking alternately serious and bemused, and then a "two-shot" of the two of them speaking, which would be accompanied on camera by voice-over. It was a lot of work for less than two minutes of airtime.

"So, what makes chocolate so romantic?" Rose asked, after carefully adjusting his horn-rims.

"Actually, it's not just chocolate," said the professor, an attractive and well-coiffed woman in her late forties—about my age, in fact. "A study published in the *Journal of Social and Personal Relationships* in 2015 found that eating something sweet can lead to heightened feelings of romance. The participants in the study who were single were more likely to imagine positive romantic relationships after tasting sweets."

"Like Godiva chocolates?" Rose grinned.

Kalashnikov smiled back. "Actually, the study used Oreo mini-cookies, but the principle is the same."

I made a mental note to pull out some quotes from this for the section of *Ben*, our quarterly alumni magazine, which features faculty members in the news.

"And what about roses?" Rose asked. I smiled a bit, thinking of the bouquet in the vase on Popcorn's desk; I hadn't thought Oscar had it in him.

"Not just roses but red roses in particular have always been associated with love, all the way back to Greek mythology. The color red itself can mean many things—war, courage, anger, and religious fervor as well as love. But it is always associated with passion."

Speaking of passion, Mac and I dropped in on Banfield in her office after the interview and found her going over the Williams case with Gibbons. Their idea of a hot date! They've also been known to indulge in archery and dodgeball together. The expedition to campus police (SBUP) headquarters on the lower level of Physical Plant was my idea, to which Mac had assented with seeming reluctance.

"I am really questioning my ability to help in this case, old boy," he sighed, "given my failure in our last outing."

"Lent is only two weeks away," I said. "Offer it up."

Hours of tedious legwork had left Banfield fresh as a daisy, whereas I got exhausted just listening to her report:

"Along with the other officers, we're looking at more than two thousand, three hundred participants in the Expo."

"You couldn't possibly interview that many in two days!" I objected.

"We didn't," Gibbons said. "And won't."

"We took their names," Banfield clarified. "Now we're going through their social media accounts to get photos from the Expo and see what they've posted about Williams in the past."

"Well done!" Mac rumbled.

"We need to get CCTV in there like on all those British cop shows," Banfield said.

SBU has surveillance, but not to the extent of larger universities and not at the Towne Center. I made a mental note to contact Cal Daley and Ed Decker to suggest stepping up their game on that, then mentally tore it up because I knew that Banfield would be on that.

"We made a few notes," she said, swinging her laptop our way so we could see what she'd written. "In alphabetical order. Men are included on the theory that 'woman' and 'red' could be two different people. Or a man dressed as a woman. And, obviously, this doesn't include people who paid in cash at the door and left before the crime scene was secured." *In other words, there's a hole big enough to drive Mac's car through.*

I'll just give you a sampling in Banfield's words, skipping all but one of the thirty-six Red Falcons who turned out to be innocent, and giving you only one woman dressed in the red costume of a relatively obscure male superhero:

Women

Burton, Shalimar—media influencer with strawberry blonde hair, red nails and lipstick; her posts on Pinterest show that she didn't like Parker Williams but is a big fan of Alexandra Hale.

Crowley, Tamsin—an actress popular in films 40 years ago who now voices Captain Zero in an animated cartoon; famous for her red scarves, which all began with a *Vogue* cover in which she wasn't wearing much else.

DeVries, Helen—dressed as a female version of the male character Red Raven (a costume with wings); has a social media history of very negative comments about the male-dominated comic book world.

Hale, Alexandra—a black comic book artist in a red jumper.

Hollander, Sandy—an Erin resident dressed as Red Falcon who frequently proclaimed on Twitter her passion for the work of Parker Williams; a thwarted passion?

Men

Chase, Llewellyn—an actor dressed in a ridiculously red shirt.

Frost-Pierson, Gavin—known antagonist of the victim; wore a red baseball cap before and after the murder.

Lumpkin, Bobby—employee of the sponsoring Graphic Images; was wearing a Cincinnati Reds jacket as he left the Expo on Saturday and could have been earlier.[10]

O'Connor, Richard "Red"—his hair is mostly gray, but Red is still his nickname. (Largely cleared by Chief Hummel.)

Spargo, Rasputin—a comic book collector wearing a big red tie.

"A veritable red tide of suspects!" Mac observed, proving that he has no shame.

My take was a little different:

"Do you see any real possibilities there? Somebody with the motive and the nerve to commit a murder with thousands of potential witnesses nearby? I don't. I hate to say this, but even Frost-Pierson doesn't look good for it, unless it

[10] But he wasn't when I saw him.—*T.J.C*

turns out he had no chance of wringing money out of a living Parker Williams. And besides, Williams knew it was Frost-Pierson beneath that red cap and could have named him." *As Mac pointed out.*

"Williams's phone shows that he had a number of phone calls with the Spargo guy and an appointment with somebody named Graham Bentley Post the day he died," Gibbons reported.

Post? I know that name!

Mac raised an eyebrow. "Mr. Frost-Pierson picked up Mr. Spargo's card on Saturday as a potential buyer for some comics he hopes to sell."

"That lets this Spargo guy out," I said. "Remember, Frost-Pierson said he was on the second floor at the time we know the murder must have happened."

The McCabe synapses fired quickly. "Perhaps we have the scenario all wrong. It is not impossible that Mr. Spargo—having murder on his mind—encountered Parker Williams alone in the second-floor hallway, stabbed his victim, shoved the body into the elevator, sent that elevator downstairs, then quickly returned to the table where he was offering to purchase collectables. Under that scenario, Rebecca then entered the hallway and pushed the button bringing the elevator back up before the doors even opened on the first floor."

"And what do you figure the chances of that?" Banfield asked.

"About as great as Mac's chances of winning the Flying Pig marathon," I suggested.

"Approximately so," Mac granted. "Still, Mr. Spargo remains a suspect, however unlikely. A man whose first name is 'Rasputin' cannot be disregarded. As to Graham Bentley

Post, Jefferson and I met him during our first murder inves-tigation eleven years ago.[11] He is director of the Library & Museum of Popular Culture, based in Brattleboro, Vermont. I did not observe him at the Expo, however."

"We don't know that he was there," Banfield said. "He and Williams were supposed to meet at seven o'clock Saturday for dinner at Ricoletti's."

"We need to check," Gibbons said.

"Copy that."

"If Williams knew those guys, he would have had no reason to identify either of them by the color of something he was wearing," I said. "That's the argument against Frost-Pierson as the killer, isn't it?"

"Maybe Williams didn't know Spargo and/or Post by sight," Gibbons said.

"And even if he did," Mac tossed in, "the killer could have been wearing a mask or costume that was much more concealing than Mr. Frost-Pierson's baseball cap."

"Oh."

My head thumped.

Mac's phone rang. He looked to see who was calling. Instead of answering with a jaunty, "Sebastian McCabe here," he said, "Hello, Oscar," and put the call on speakerphone. "How goes the battle?"

"It's a slog," the Chief replied. "That pesky Felicity Snow showed up and asked what's going on with her client. I told her to read the *Observer.*"

"I hope her paper got delivered," I said.

Oscar ignored me. "I'm going to talk to the widow at three-thirty this afternoon in her room at the Harridan. She

---

[11] See *No Police Like Holmes* (MX Publishing, 2011).

says she'll be busy until then with matters pertaining to her husband's untimely demise, like the funeral, the will, and such. She's flying in her personal assistant to help her with all that. Anyway, do you want to go along?"

"I am not certain that—" Mac began.

"Sure," I said, knowing that's what GK would want. "We'll meet you at your office."

IT WAS A SURPRISE to see our next-door neighbor, Ginger Ronson-Patch, cutting back some flowering bush in front of her house when I went home for lunch—and not only because I didn't know February is the time to do that. I expected her to be in her office on Cherry Street. Ginger's work as a physiotherapist really took off after the pandemic because of so many people getting neck strains from leaning over laptops at Zoom conferences.

"I decided to give myself a mental health day," Ginger said. "Aaron is having a hard time with that murder on Saturday."

The Cody memory banks kicked in. "He was there, wasn't he? At the Expo."

She nodded solemnly. "My sweet husband's always been a comic book fan. He was kind of freaked out at having to give his name to the cops before he left that afternoon."

"Just routine," I assured her.

After some small talk (the Patches didn't get their paper either), I went into the Cody manse half-expecting to be assailed by the twins upon entering. But they weren't there—just my Valentine. She didn't say anything by way of greeting. Her lips were otherwise occupied.

She was dressed to the nines in her curve-hugging silk LBD (little black dress), dangling silver earrings, and the brooch I'd given her that morning. Her lips and nails were Valentine-red. She'd done up her curly, honey-blonde hair in a French twist and applied an inebriating dose of Cleopatra VII perfume. Three-inch heels brought her up to my height, which had its advantages.

The dining room table was laden down with a slap-up pasta meal, at which the half-Italian Lynda excels. The waiting meal was kept company by lit candles and a bottle of Roadhouse Red from Erin's own Silk Stocking Winery—a rare indulgence at lunch for two people with three children aged six and under.

"I know this isn't exactly health food," she said after the blessing.

"No, it's not," I agreed, "but it's doing wonders for my mental health."

We talked about the Williams case, which led me to ask Lynda—after the second glass of Roadhouse Red—why she stopped dating Gavin Pierson, as he was then known. She said something about how he was a fine fellow, but a bit in-secure and the sparks weren't there.

"I guess I was waiting for you, darling," she said in summary, her husky voice at its huskiest. "I just didn't know it at the time."

"Well, I'm glad you did," I understated. "Wait for me, I mean."

"You mean you're happy I proposed?"

And so forth.

Twenty minutes later I surveyed the wreckage on the table, including a nearly empty wine bottle, and patted my stomach. "Well, this has been a wonderful Valentine's Day, my love, but I guess I'd better get back to the office." *Not that I want to.*

Lynda bent over, way over, and blew out the candles. "Office? Oh, I don't think so, *tesoro mio.*"

Chapter Ten
Red Death

POPCORN MADE A production number out of looking at her watch when I finally got back to the Gamble Building. "Long lunch."

"Something came up. But I'll make up for it by leaving early. In about an hour Mac and I are accompanying your gentleman friend to the hotel suite of a beautiful Hollywood star."

She didn't bite. Maybe the vase of red roses on her desk from I Knew Who made her impervious to my attempts to awaken the green-eyed monster.

I spent a few minutes online reading Morrie Kindle's story about student debt, which spelled my name right, then huddled with Sylvester Link for half an hour about the looming deadline for *Ben*. It was his first issue as editor and primary writer of the magazine. GK may be reviled by faculty for some of his budget-cutting moves, but he has also expanded staff judiciously in view of SBU's growing size. One such move was the recent addition of Link on a contract basis. In time it might become a staff job.

"I'm sure you understand that in the light of weekend events we have to postpone your cover story on SBU Towne Center and the interview with Dr. Nelan," I told him.

"Yeah, I figured that was coming," said Link, a black man in his early thirties with a thin mustache. "How about if we go with the story that I had scheduled for the fall issue about the criminal justice studies program? It's moving up to the status of a department, you know, and its students are interning at eleven different agencies and initiatives this semester."

One of those initiatives was the Ohio Innocence Project. That recalled to my mind media influencer Shalimar Burton, the Comic Expo participant freed from prison through the Innocence Project efforts of Mini Cooper. But I didn't linger over the thought.

"Good idea," I said. "Make it happen."

Link nodded, not sparing a smile, and made a note on his phone. Not for nothing did I call him "Serious Sylvester" back when he was a student reporter for *The Spectator* a decade earlier. After graduating from SBU, Link worked at the *St. Louis Post-Dispatch* for several years until he got caught in a round of layoffs—just like Gavin Frost-Pierson and thousands of other journalists over the past two decades. He'd come back to Erin a bit bruised by life and needing to balance other contract jobs with this one to make ends meet (including adjunct instructor of journalism and *Spectator* advisor). But he still wore his signature khakis, sport coat, and staid demeanor.

As we discussed other stories ("Recent Grads Report Great Success") and standing features ("Class Notes," "In Memory Of," "Where Are You Reading *Ben*?") for the spring edition of the alumni mag, my mind wandered to what Valentina Kalashnikov said to Brian Rose about red as the color of passion. No, I wasn't thinking about my lunchtime with Lynda. I was thinking that shoving a stiletto or whatever it was into Parker Williams's heart certainly sounded like a crime of passion—a very red death with no masque involved—and yet, if Mac was right, the murder was premeditated.

". . . and I was contemplating adding a new feature pulling positive alumni statements about SBU from social media," Link said. "What do you think?"

"I think it's a great idea. Do it! I have to get going now, Sylvester. Professor McCabe and I are going to posse up with Chief Hummel soon to talk with somebody in connection with the Williams murder." *That somebody being the widow, who is usually the most likely suspect, although probably not in this case. But wait! Now that I think about it—*

"Maybe I can find a new angle for a story about Professor McCabe in *Ben*," Link said.

"A new angle? I doubt it, but you can try."

OUR ART DECO police station still carries the inscription "Fifth National Bank of Erin" in the sandstone above the pillars on the front of the building, a seldom-noticed memory of a financial institution long ago merged into Gamble Bank. We arrived there in plenty of time to meet up with Oscar and walk the short distance from Court Street to the Harridan Hotel on nearby Front Street, locally famed for its expansive views of the Ohio River from the upper rooms and outdoor terrace.

Holly Burdette, Oscar's young executive assistant with pixie-cut copper hair and a penchant for pearl earrings, greeted us with her usual bounce and verve, followed by: "You just missed Rebecca. She came in to give her formal statement. Now the Chief's in the conference room with Mr. Frost-Pierson and his lawyer. He said to go on in."

Mac raised an eyebrow in surprise. This party we had not expected.

The conference room is in what used to be the bank's vault. If you think that's a cute idea, thank you. I had to talk Oscar into it. Gathered around the table when we entered were Oscar, Felicity Snow, and Gavin Frost-Pierson. The lawyer, who appeared to be giving Erica Slade a run for her money in the line of criminal defense work, was saying:

"That's hardly illegal."

Oscar had his mouth open to reply as we entered.

"I hope we are not intruding," Mac said.

"Have a seat," the Chief said. "I would have called, but I figured you were already on your way when my guests arrived. Holly found something very interesting that required me to have a chat with Mr. Frost-Pierson. Remember those veiled death threats against him on Facebook? Don't ask me how, but Holly figured out with her computer skills that this fine citizen posted them himself, using a fake account."

Holly is almost terminally cute and therefore easy to underestimate—as Frost-Pierson just learned, if he was paying attention. I had doubts about that.

"My idea was that I could gin up some sympathy that way," he said, sounding sullen. Something about his eyes reminded me of a dog who'd just been scolded.

"Bad idea," Oscar said. "In fact, the word 'stupid' comes to mind."

"Perhaps so," Snow acknowledged, "but hardly criminal. And surely this unwise but not illegal action demonstrates that my client doesn't have the intellectual capacity to murder someone without being caught on the spot."

Ah, the old stupidity defense!

"The ploy also calls into question his honesty, and therefore the veracity of all his statements," Mac wanted her to know.

Snow stood up and looped a purse over her shoulder. "Are we finished here, Chief?"

Oscar directed his response to Frost-Pierson. "You can go for now. I have your number."

Did Oscar intend a double meaning with his parting shot? Probably not.

"It's been a pleasure," the attorney said on her way out.

OSCAR UPDATED US on the Banfield-Gibbons work as we walked to the Harridan for his appointment with Miranda Blackwood.

"They came up with some pretty juicy stuff," he summarized.

"So, dish," I said.

"Remember that guy with the funny name, Rasputin Spargo?"

"He was the individual buying pre-1971 comic books on the second floor of the Towne Center during the Expo," Mac said as he fired up one of his Antonio de la Cova cigars, which were incredibly expensive even before inflation took off like a rocket. "And he appears several times in Mr. Williams's phone records, according to Colonel Gibbons."

"Yeah, him. Well, get this: Four years ago, he was one of several dozen collectors around the country who bought rare comic books stolen from the Special Collections & Archives of the Elbridge Gerry University Library. The head of library security was the thief. The owners of a comic book shop in Maine got suspicious of the stuff they were being offered—rare Batman and Superman comics—and reported it to the university. The university investigated and discovered that a boatload of stuff was missing from the library, almost five thousand comic books, even though they were kept behind a chain link fence protected by a padlock. Why would a library do that, by the way? Seems excessive, although I guess it wasn't. Anyhow, Spargo claimed to be an innocent buyer, and there was no proof to the contrary, so he skated."

I vaguely remembered the case, which was reported at some length in *Higher Ed Insider.*

"What else do you know about Spargo?" I asked.

"He's loaded. Made a pile as an early investor in cryptocurrency, then got out before it went down the toilet. Now he's soaking up the market in rare and valuable comic books, whatchamacallits—"

"Graphic novels?"

"Yeah, them, and also the original artwork," Oscar continued. "He's never had any other brush with the law, not even regulators."

"Nonetheless, his receipt of stolen goods is worthy of note," Mac said.

"Right. It's fishy. And so is that guy Red O'Connor, by the way. What we didn't know when we talked to him on Saturday is that his name came up last year in relation to a forged piece of *Amazing Spider-Man* cover art. The real thing was drawn back in the 1960s by somebody named Ditko, apparently a star, and is mega-valuable."

"That is unsurprising," Mac said. "Just last month artist Mike Zeck's 1984 black and white drawing of Spider-Man's costume being consumed by an alien symbiote—thus explaining the origin of the superhero's mysterious black costume—sold at auction for well over three million dollars. That was ten times the expected price and a new record for comic book art."

The only part of that I understood was "three million dollars."

"But anyway," Oscar persisted, "the art I'm talking about got outed as a fake when the real thing turned up in the hands of a private collector. It was apparently a big game in that world trying to figure out whodunit—but the number one suspect was O'Connor, who once worked on *Spider-Man* and had a bad parting. Of course, that's just—"

Oscar's phone rang. "Oh, fruitcake." He didn't really say 'fruitcake.' "It's Rawls calling again. And I've already had Morrie Kindle from the AP, PNN's Bennington Lee, Joe Ziebart at the *Cincinnati Sentinel*, and two Cincinnati TV stations on my ass today."

"Tell Johanna I didn't get my *Observer* this morning," I said.

He didn't do so, nor did he give her a chance to ask a question.

"The investigation by the Erin and St. Benignus University police forces into the murder of Parker Williams is ongoing," he said by way of greeting. "We have no higher priority. But we are still in the early stage of our inquiries. Therefore, we have made no arrests and as of yet there are no persons of interest. What else can I tell you?"

"Hello to you, too, Chief," I could hear the reporter say. "Did you get the autopsy results? I haven't been able to reach the coroner."

"I spoke to Dr. Eppensteiner about an hour ago and she confirmed that the victim was stabbed through the heart with a thin blade, although, technically, she can't yet say that was actually the cause of death."

But he didn't die of the flu.

"Have you talked to the victim's wife, Miranda Blackwood?"

"That will happen shortly as a matter of routine."

Shortly was an understatement. We were less than a block from the hotel.

Chapter Eleven
Red Woman

AFTER OSCAR disconnected from the local press, he informed us, "Oh, and the mayor called, too. He wants me to tread lightly so as to avoid bad publicity for Erin on a national scale in view of the Blackwood angle, her being an A-list actress and all."

This is going to be like juggling egg whites, and just as sticky.

"Good luck with that," I said. "We're here to help. Do you really think there's any chance a Hollywood type would kill a spouse instead of just divorcing him?"

"Are you kidding?" Oscar fired back. "There's a whole documentary on *The Twenty Most Horrifying Hollywood Murders.* Popcorn loved it."

This last was uttered just as we entered the elegant lobby of the Harridan—whereupon we saw two men engaged in a heated exchange. The one in his early sixties, wearing a tailored blue suit, I recognized as Graham Bentley Post, although his hair and mustache were grayer than they'd been eleven years earlier. "You, sir, will regret this!" he sputtered.

"I doubt it," said his antagonist, who was younger than me but dressed like an Edwardian dandy, right down to the black suit and vest, and the walking stick that he brandished in two hands as if it were a sword. He even sported a

Vandyke beard, dishwater blond in color, and wore a red tie, although Mac subsequently called it a foulard.

One of the front desk receptionists, whom I knew casually, told me later that the pair had been engaging in this verbal duel for five or ten minutes before we arrived.

"Greetings, gentlemen!" Mac hailed the disputants.

The younger, looking startled, lowered his walking stick.

"He's no gentleman," Post objected. "He's Rasputin Spargo, and he's here to prey upon a new widow at her most vulnerable. And aren't you Sebastian McCabe?"

"Guilty, Mr. Post! You know Jefferson Cody, of course, and this is Chief Oscar Hummel of the Erin Police Department. We are here to speak with Ms. Blackwood about the death of her husband."

"So are we, in a way," Spargo said, throwing a contemptuous glance Post's way. He leaned on his walking stick, the top of which was a brass eagle head with diamond eyes— much fancier than the one Mac occasionally carries.

Post assumed an air of offended dignity. "It's true that I hope to speak to Ms. Blackwood about acquiring some of Parker Williams's collection of valuable comic art for the Library & Museum of Popular Culture. He and I had been in serious discussions about that before his tragic death. Of course, his own work is much more valuable now that he's gone, and I am prepared to pay accordingly."

Cold!

"More valuable?" Oscar said. "Is that so?"

"It's a simple matter of supply and demand. When a creator of art dies, the supply has reached its maximum. When it comes to collectibles of almost any kind, limited supply creates increased demand—and pushes the price up."

I remembered reading a story about that concept just a few weeks earlier in *The Wall Street Journal* with regard to the recent passing of a number of pop artists. It didn't refer to comic book cover art, but there was no reason the principle wouldn't apply there. I made a mental note to tell Ashley Crutcher that Williams's sketch of Red Falcon, executed for her on the spot at that Poisoned Pens meeting, should be either framed or put in her safe deposit box. Was Ashley at the Expo? I couldn't recall seeing her there.

"But Parker never would have sold to Post," Spargo said, "because he knew that the Library & Museum of Popular Culture has had a forgery on display for the past two months."

"What forgery?" Post sputtered.

"That cover of the first issue of *She-Wolf*."

"Don't be absurd!"

"She-Wolf?" Oscar echoed.

"A female Native American anti-hero," Spargo informed him (and me). "The publication launched in 1971, right at the dawn of the Bronze Age of Comics." *And the year Mac was born!*

"Curious," She-Wolf's age cohort mused. "It used to be acceptable to refer to a Native American male as a red man. Therefore, a Native American female might be said to be a red woman."

"As in WOMAN RED?" I interpreted. "Are you kidding? That brainstorm puts the far in far-fetched."

"I am merely processing out loud, old boy."

Sometimes I hate extroverts.

"However, I would also point out that the character wears a red costume, to the extent to which she is clothed at all," Mac added.

"But the She-Wolf art on display in Brattleboro is not the real thing," Spargo said, dragging us back to the topic at hand, and to reality. "And Parker knew that because *he* has the real thing."

"And how do you supposedly know that?" Post huffed.

"That doesn't matter."

"You're just jealous because a number of collectors have seen fit to donate or will their collections to the Library & Museum because they knew we will be good stewards. Such works should be available to all, not held for private enjoyment by wealthy individuals."

I thought: *You mean individuals like the ones who donated them to you?*

Spargo snorted.

Oscar regarded the dandy. "You're not exactly in a position to get on your high horse about honest dealings, Spargo."

I noticed Spargo's hand tighten its grip on his swanky walking stick. "What's that supposed to mean?"

He'd have been better off not playing dumb; it made him look like he had something to hide, which he did.

"You know what he means," Post said. "Everybody in the comic world knows about the thefts from the Elbridge Gerry University Library. How many of the four thousand, nine hundred and twelve stolen comics did you get caught with?"

Spargo's face turned red. "How was I supposed to know they were stolen?"

"Actually, it was not all that difficult," Mac rumbled. "It took me just five minutes to find a list of all the missing items on the University website, and that was available before you made the purchases."

"I may want to talk to both of you more later," Oscar warned them, "but right now we're running late for an appointment with Ms. Blackwood."

"I'll go with you," Post and Spargo said, more or less in synch.

"No way."

Chapter Twelve

Red Ring

"BERTSCH FOUND the widow here at the hotel when she came to give her the bad news," Oscar said as we rode the elevator up to the 23rd floor. I'm not sure I'll ever feel the same about elevators again after seeing Williams's body in one, but it beat walking the stairs. "She'd already ordered a cab to take her to the Towne Center for her panel at six o'clock. So, nothing suspicious there. I think this is going to be a dry hole."

"If the spouse is the first suspect, and she is not a likely one, surely previous spouses are worth a look," Mac said, almost off-handedly.

"And Williams had two of them," I tossed in.

"With the combined vast resources of the Erin and SBU forces being what they are," Oscar said, laying it on with a trowel, "and the exes not being high on my list of likely assassins, we'll get to them eventually. At this point I don't even know their names."

A bodyguard type answered the door of Miranda Blackwood's suite. The young man had marine-short sandy hair and arms like telephone poles sticking out of a polo shirt.

"I'm Kyle Rufus, Ms. Blackwood's personal assistant," he explained.

Something about that name rang a bell, but I hadn't the foggiest notion what it was. The PA led us into a room half the size of Delaware, elegantly appointed with real paintings and handsome furniture. It was the Harridan's presidential suite, although no president (at least not of the United States) had ever stayed there. I guess it was at that point that Rufus silently disappeared, although I didn't notice his absence until later. My attention was otherwise occupied. Miranda Blackwood sat perched on a sofa longer than Mac's Chevy, wearing a floral pleated skirt that showed off notable lower limbs. You know what she looked like: beautiful, and well aware of it, with wide green eyes and a full mouth. She was the Red Falcon of the movies, except that her natural hair color was auburn, not black.

"Thank you for agreeing to see us," Oscar said. It would be unfair to say he was star-struck, having already interviewed two actresses on Saturday, but his demeanor was markedly deferential—in sharp contrast to his approach with the sparring duo downstairs. "We know how difficult this is, ma'am, and we are sorry for your loss."

"Thank you. I appreciate that. But I have to say I wasn't expecting a delegation, Officer."

Ignoring the demotion, the Chief doled out our names and explained, "I'm sure you want us to find your husband's killer as soon as possible. These gentlemen have been of help to the police along those lines in the past."

Without commenting on that, our hostess waved us into any of the numerous chairs dotting the room. As she did so I noticed that she was wearing a ruby ring on her right hand. Red was everywhere in this case! But I'm pretty sure, based on previous conversations with Holly Burdette, that

Oscar's executive assistant would call that confirmation bias: She'd say I saw red because I was looking for it, and then I was reading meaning into it where there wasn't any. And maybe she'd be right. Or maybe not.

"Forgive me for asking the obvious," Oscar said upon sitting, "but do you know of anyone who would want to kill your husband?"

She didn't take any time to chew that over. "I assume you mean other than that awful man who accused Parker of stealing Queen Bee." She shook her head. "No, all I can think is that it was some deranged woman with a grievance, real or imagined, dressed as Red Falcon." Clearly, and understandably, she'd read about her husband's dying message. "But I have to admit that I didn't know much about his life here in Erin. It's not something we talked about much."

"Why not?"

"Why would we?"

Ouch.

"How was his relationship with his previous wives?"

"There was none, so far as I know."

"May I ask why you and Mr. Williams chose to live apart?" Mac asked.

"I assume you just did. What does that have to do with his murder?"

"In all probability, nothing at all. We are seeking to learn as much as we can about the deceased, beyond what we already know. Jefferson and I met him on two occasions."

Blackwood crossed her lovely legs, her wide green eyes looking beyond us and into the past.

"I've been a big fan of Red Falcon since I was in college, and I was totally jazzed to play the part; that's not just studio publicity. I was almost equally eager to meet her creator. That happened on the set of the first Red Falcon movie three years ago. We married within three months. He was sixteen years older than me, but that didn't matter. What attracted me was his confidence. He had all the self-possession of a pirate. And best of all, he wasn't an actor.

"I'd been married before, not successfully, but I decided to give it another try as long as I could do it on my terms. I already had a life in Malibu with my son that I didn't want to change. As it happened, Parker had a studio here in Ohio where he was comfortable. So, we married but each of us stayed where we were. He visited me a lot, in California or on location, and we Zoomed in between. I was only here in Erin once before, incognito; this time I stayed here at the Harridan under my own name and Parker stayed with me. There were no strains in our relationship, if that's what you're fishing for."

Mac pooh-poohed the very thought. "I assure you, Ms. Blackwood, I restrict my fishing to a tributary of the Ohio River. However, it would be remiss of me not to note that Winsome Lerouge was asked at the panel on Saturday about her relationships with you and your husband."

"Supermarket tabloid stuff!" Winsome had used almost the same phrasing, but the words "supermarket" and "tabloid" do seem made for each other. "Look, the only thing coming between Winsome and me is her ego. She can't get over the fact that she's been around awhile." *Meow!* Winsome was all of about thirty-five, and more beautiful than ever in my book. "Her agent probably planted those rumors about her and Parker so that she could deny them."

Meanwhile, I was thinking maybe Blackwood's son didn't think everything was so hunky-dory at home.

"Your son—" I tried.

"Is seven years old," she snapped. "Leave Elias out of this. I've tried very hard to protect him."

Cowed, I retreated to my mobile—and texted Kelly Richards: *Who fathered Miranda Blackwood's son?* I figured that would be faster than doing a search on the TMZ website.

"This conversation is reminding me that I'll have to sell Parker's place," the widow mused. I remembered it as a mid-century modern split level, circa late 1950s or early 1960s, and the biggest house of that lamentable architectural style that I'd ever seen. "That will take a while. He'd lived there so long there will be a lot to clear out—his own artwork and his collection."

"We ran into two guys downstairs who'll be happy to help with that," Oscar said. He explained about Post and Spargo.

"The vultures! I'll make sure they don't get any of it."

Nobody knows, Richards texted back. *Big secret.*

I flirted with the idea that Blackwood's bodyguard-esque PA, Kyle Rufus, might be the lucky man. But in that case, he wouldn't still be hanging around, would he? Or maybe he would, given that Hollywood types were involved. And what was there about his name that was bugging me?

"Selling Parker's house should be no problem," I told Blackwood. "It's a seller's market right now. A real estate agent I know tells me that it's become a blood sport. Buyers are offering all kinds of incentives to get a leg up on other bidders, from naming their first-born child after the seller to a year's worth of Winter's ice cream."

I had no clue that just three months later, with mortgage interest rates soaring, that wouldn't be the case.

"What's your friend's name?"

"Cecily Almond, of Happy Homes Realty. I highly recommend her. She was the selling agent when my wife and I bought our home."

This was no time to mention that there was a dead body in the freezer when we first looked at the place.[12]

"I'll have Kyle call her," Blackwood said.

"UNDOUBTEDLY YOU noticed that ruby ring on her finger," Mac told Oscar as we rode down in the elevator.

"You mean the ring that her dying husband would have recognized even if she was wearing a fully concealing costume, so that he would know who she was and would have given her name instead of an obscure clue—that ring?"

This verbal barrage left Mac unfazed. "You assume too much, Oscar. The late Mr. Williams might not have recognized the ring if it were a recent acquisition, perhaps a gift from a male admirer."

---

[12] See "A Cold Case" in *Rogues Gallery* (MX Publishing, 2014).

Chapter Thirteen
Red Tide

"WHAT YOU CALLED A red tide of suspects has kind of washed out," Banfield told Mac back at the police station.

As she was speaking, he removed his ceramic **I SEE NO REASON TO ACT MY AGE** mug from Oscar's Keurig machine, brimming with caffeine-laced coffee. The big guy French presses his freshly-ground beans at home but knows how to rough it without complaint.

"How so, Aurelia?"

"Let's start with motive, Seb—or, rather, lack thereof. The victim's phone doesn't show texted threats or heated exchanges with anybody on our list."

"What about just the opposite—expressions of un-dying love that might lead to a *crime passionnel?*" Mac asked.

I wouldn't have believed that Banfield was capable of blushing if I hadn't seen it for myself. "Well, there were some pretty smoldering text messages with photos attached, but they were from his wife."

Moving right along . . .

"What about social media?" Oscar asked.

"Shalimar Burton admitted that on Saturday morning she posted on Facebook and subsequently deleted a photo of

Williams holding court at the Towne Center, accompanied by a nasty message," Gibbons said.

"What was the message?"

"She called him a, quote, 'supershit.'" *Nice play on her "superbabe" theme!*

"That negativity seems highly uncharacteristic from what we know of Ms. Burton," Mac said.

"Right. Normally, she's all sunshine and roses. That's her gig as a social media influencer, mostly on Twitter and Instagram. She said she lost her head with that Facebook post because Williams mistreated a friend of hers, whom she refused to name for fear of casting suspicion on said friend. Burton claims she never actually met the man and the only time she even saw him was Saturday morning in the big hall at the SBU Towne Center right before she sent the message. We didn't fully investigate that . . ."

"Because she has a strong alibi," Banfield said. "She was hanging out with a woman named Alexandra Hale during the entire window when Williams could have been killed."

"Maybe they were in it together," I posited.

"Extremely unlikely, given that Hale and Williams were friends. They exchanged several texts in the days before the Expo. And get your mind out of the gutter, Seb." Mac had the grace to look chastened. "I said 'friends.' They were like 'it's been too long' and 'it will be good to catch up,' that kind of thing."

"Go on," Oscar directed, his head resting on his right palm. "What about the women in red costumes? They seem promising."

"They did," Gibbons said, with a slight accent on the past tense.

"Right," Banfield said. "Helen DeVries was gender-bendingly dressed as Red Raven, a fairly obscure Marvel Comics character. It gets a little complicated because there were three different characters of that name, one of which was a woman. But her costume was the original Red Raven, who was male and had big wings. She made it herself."

"It was hard to miss," I recalled from Saturday morning.

"Anyhoo, as to motive, it's true that Ms. DeVries has been quite vocal on social media about Williams's penchant for drawing, let's say, very well-endowed women. But he's not exactly unique in that regard." I thought of Captain Marvel, then I thought of Lynda as Captain Marvel, then I had to pull my mind back to the subject at hand. Banfield went on: "If our Red Raven tried to kill every comic artist she called out on social media as a purveyor of toxic masculinity, she'd have to give up her day job as a kindergarten aide."

"One could argue that she had to start somewhere," Mac said, obviously not believing it.

"Then there's Sandy Hollander, who was dressed as Red Falcon herself," Banfield said. "She's on the other end of the spectrum—thought Parker Williams was 'the greatest thing since Stan Lee and Jack Kirby rolled into one.' Whatever that means. But she says the only time she met him was that morning when she commissioned a sketch, and that seems plausible. She's a shy woman of about fifty, a teacher married to an engineer. I guess in theory she could have met Williams in that hallway and made a rejected advance that ended disastrously. You know what they say about the quiet ones. But there's one more thing that rules out both DeVries and Hollander."

"The weapon," Gibbons supplied before I could guess. "Since we didn't find a discarded blade anywhere in the Towne Center, the killer must have taken it away. Both of the women we're talking about were still in the building when we shut it down, and both were searched."

"Actually, that applies to everybody who was on our suspect list," Banfield said. "And they all fail the motive test as well, so far as we know. The actors Tamsin Crowley and Llewellyn Chase, for example, had no known connection to Williams. We can dig deeper into that later, if necessary, but they aren't low-hanging fruit."

Ignoring the mixed metaphor, Mac asked, "What about Bobby Lumpkin?"

"Also searched," Gibbons said.

"Plus, he's another case of no clear motive," Banfield added. "Although they had to have known each other, it's not obvious how Lumpkin profits from Williams's death. But, who knows, there could be some weird romance angle or revenge from some slight that we don't know about."

And so forth.

"What about your interview with the widow?" Banfield asked Oscar after fruitlessly kicking around a few more non-starters from the Banfield-Gibbons suspect list.

"Nothing that touched off my Spidey-sense." *Puh-leeze!* "She didn't pour on the tears. If she'd done that, I'd have been a mite suspicious, seeing as how she's a top-level actress. Which reminds me, Williams may have been rolling in dough, but not enough to make inheritance a motive, given his wife's multi-million-dollar movie contracts."

"I should note that Ms. Blackwood wears a red ring, a ruby, on her right hand," Mac said. "In theory, it could have been given to her by a paramour, therefore unknown to her husband, and it could have been the only thing she was wearing that was not an identity-concealing costume as she stabbed Mr. Williams, thereby eliciting his dying message of "woman" and "red."

"Bullshit," Oscar judged.

"I said, 'in theory.'" Mac sounded hurt. "And I have re-thought that theory since first voicing it in the elevator at the Harridan. Motive is lacking for Ms. Blackwood. According to my online research last night when I could not sleep, the only romantic gossip surrounding her is the notion that Winsome Lerouge was enamored of her husband—which both she and Ms. Lerouge reject. And surely if there were such a triangle, the homicide of the object of their mutual affection would not be the way to resolve it. Divorce would settle the matter nicely." He shook his massive head. "No, that will not do. And the text message trail between Mr. Williams and his spouse, as reported by Aurelia, only supports Ms. Blackwood's assertion that they were a happy couple."

Oscar moved along, filling in Banfield and Gibbons about our encounter with Spargo and Post.

"What do you think about those two strange birds?" he asked Mac at the end.

"The stench of acquisitiveness and greed clings to both of them," Mac said. "My instinct tells me that we will have occasion to speak with them again."

Oscar grunted.

"By the way," I said, "happy Valentine's Day, everybody!"

Banfield stole a glance at Gibbons, who reciprocated with all the emotion of Lincoln's face on Mount Rushmore.

It had been a long day—although the visit home at noon was delightful—and I was looking forward to a quiet night at home with Lynda and the kids.

But I didn't get one.

Chapter Fourteen
Red-Handed

"ONE FOR YOU, Mommy." Donata handed a Valentine's card to Lynda. "And one for you, Daddy. I made them at school. I already gave Andy his." Andy Patch, son of Ginger and Aaron next door, is her best friend and classmate.

Sam and Jake, not to be outdone, proffered their efforts along the same lines. "Open mine first." "No, mine." Lynda and I each opened one. It was a wonderfully sane departure from an afternoon of spitballing murder theories.

Dinner was light compared to lunch—small portions of heart-healthy grilled salmon with a honey bourbon glaze and a vegetable medley on the side—but topped off with a red velvet cake in the shape of a heart.

I was halfway through a rather substantial serving of the unhealthful but luscious dessert when a text popped up on my mobile. *Incoming!* As a matter of principle, I hate the idea of being always available, but that's part of my job description and I hate the idea of unemployment even more. No quiet quitting for a communications director!

But it wasn't work. At least, not SBU work. It was Mac, telling me: *We are needed. I will pick you up in 10 minutes.*

His tone annoyed me, so I responded: *Says who?*

Al Daponte. I shall explain as I drive. I like this no more than you do.

"What makes Mac think I'll drop everything and come running just because he says so?" I fumed to Lynda.

She rolled her eyes, which are brown flecked with gold. "I'll wait up."

"TWO ELDERLY INDIVIDUALS, one of each sex, attempted to break into Graphic Images tonight," Mac informed me as I slid into the death seat of his Chevy. "Apparently they failed to notice that Mr. Daponte lives in an apartment above the store."

"And how do we fit in?"

"The miscreants informed him that they are friends of mine, somehow thinking that would make a difference."

"Who could—oh, no! Mary Lou and Roscoe?"

"Precisely, old boy! You will recall seeing them at the Expo on Saturday. I strongly suspect that this venture into housebreaking is somehow connected to an ill-advised attempt to solve the murder."

Not only did Mary Lou Springfield think she was a mystery writer, hence her membership in the Poisoned Pens, she was also occasionally under the illusion she was the gray-haired author/sleuth from *Murder, She Wrote*. Which is strange because she writes more like Ross Macdonald. She's had the equally geriatric Roscoe Feldman wrapped around her arthritic finger since the George W. Bush administration, but rumor has it that he's slow to commit.

GRAPHIC IMAGES IS located on College Street, a few doors down from Myrtle White's Glam Gurlz hair and nail salon on the edge of downtown. The store had closed some hours earlier, and the racks and racks of colorful comic books looked a little spooky with only one light on.

"Not exactly ace cat burglars, these two," Daponte told Mac shortly after we arrived. He had one hand on each of them. "I caught them red-handed trying to get in a back window I forgot to lock sometime around September. If they'd made it in, they would have set off the burglar alarm. I don't want to press charges. Anybody can make a stupid mistake. Theirs was epically stupid, but I've had a busy day here in the store and I had enough of the cops over the weekend. I just want a responsible witness so that if they ever try anything like this again, you can verify that it wasn't the first time. That's the only reason I played along when they asked me to call you."

All of this came out in one long breath, as if he wanted to get it over with. He probably did.

Roscoe looked cowed, but then he always did. Mary Lou, who was taller and thinner with white hair instead of gray (think Miss Marple with a truncheon in her purse), had the grace to look embarrassed. That didn't last long.

Mac gave a pretty good impression of an angry parent as he addressed the culprits: "It is hard to argue with Mr. Daponte's characterization of your hapless attempt at breaking and entering. An epic mistake indeed! Surely this was the ineptest burglary since the Watergate affair. What in the world were you under the illusion you were doing?"

"Getting evidence," Roscoe spoke up, if that's what you call what he did in his hesitant voice.

Mac hiked both eyebrows. If he'd had a cigar in his mouth, it would have fallen out.

"I suppose to you it sounds silly," Mary Lou said. *Got it in one!* "But I can explain. We deduced"—Roscoe's face said *"What do you mean 'we'?"*—"that Al killed Parker Williams because Williams broke up his marriage a few years ago."

"We're back together!" Daponte exploded.

Mary Lou nodded as if that was an affirmation. "Sure, and you didn't want him messing that up."

"And the burglary?" Mac prodded.

"Technically, it only got to the level of attempted breaking and entering because we got caught before we could get in. Anyway, we—I—figured that if Williams had anything valuable on him, Al would have taken it after the murder to make a profit on the deal as well as psychological satisfaction. So that's what we were looking for—cover art or a rare comic, something like that which could be traced to ownership by Williams."

That crackbrain idea had more holes than one of Banfield's archery targets after a day of practice. I should have expected something of the sort, given the duo's lamentable attempts at detective fiction.

"Williams probably wouldn't have been just running around the Expo with an early 1970s *Spider-Man*," I said. "But if he was, and if Al took it, how would you find that particular needle in this haystack?" Sorry for the haystack metaphor again, but we were standing in the middle of a comic book store where their hypothesized "evidence," if it existed, could only have been ferreted out by an expert with tons of time on his/her hands. "And if you did find it, how could you prove that Al didn't have it legitimately? Those things don't come with a provenance, do they?" The question was addressed to Daponte, who shook his head by way of negative response.

"A lot of big money sales are done quietly," he said. "Even in auctions, sometimes names aren't used."

"In addition," Mac lectured Mary Lou, "whether the valuable item that you hypothesize was an original artwork or a supremely rare comic book, Mr. Daponte would scarcely leave it simply lying around."

"I don't have any original art at all!" Daponte exclaimed. "That's not in my line. Feel free to look, McCabe. Look, I spent twenty-five K of my own bucks on the Expo. I want it to be the start of an annual thing. The last thing I would do is kill one of the artists!"

"Well, maybe we *should* have thought this through a little better," Mary Lou conceded.

"I told you!" Roscoe told her. This sign of rebellion was surprising and encouraging. "It was that Jessica Ballantine who did it." He appealed to Mac and me. "You heard how she ripped into Williams at the Poisoned Pens meeting! She had a real mad-on for him. And she was wearing a red plaid shirt at that meeting. He probably forgot her name and 'red' was a way to identify her, whether that's what she was wearing on Saturday or not."

"I know Jessica," Daponte said with a start. "She'll buy any book with Harley Quinn as a character."

"By thunder!" Mac exclaimed. "That theory actually has the merit of being remotely credible. I did not see Ms. Ballantine on Saturday, or at least did not observe her. Did any of you?"

None of us had.

"Can we go now?" Mary Lou asked.

"Please do," the owner of the premises told her, "and don't come back."

They went.

"I guess half the town knows that Rita and Parker had a fling," Al said. *You're underestimating.* "It still hurts me, you know." Before Mac or I could even nod sympathetically, he plowed on answering questions we hadn't asked. Maybe it was therapeutic.

"They met here in the store when Parker agreed to come in and sign some of his comics. Rita was just his type—female. And I guess she was flattered by his interest. It didn't last long—a few weeks maybe—but long enough to break up his marriage to Sarah-Jane Manders, his second wife. That was more than five years ago now."

"Ms. Manders is the proprietor of Artistic Ink Tattoo Studio," Mac said.

Daponte nodded. "That's her. She was history as soon as she found out about the shenanigans with Rita, which were far from his first. I don't blame Sara-Jane for getting out, but that's not the way I roll. As I figured it, maybe I was falling down on the job as a husband. So, we hit the restart button and worked through it. Things are a lot better now, and our daughter—"

The door opened, followed by a thirty-ish, good-looking woman with light brown hair and blue eyes. Her arrival was not entirely unexpected. It was 9:20 and I knew that Rita Daponte worked at the Public Library of Erin and Sussex County, which closes at 9 P.M. on Mondays and Wednesdays, and this was a Monday. She wore a down jacket and slacks.

"Oh, you're here!" she told Daponte, although he probably knew that. "I thought you left the front light on by mistake."

"Hi, hon. This is Sebastian McCabe and Jeff Cody." He waved in our direction. "Remember, I told you they're helping the cops look into Parker's murder."

Rita Daponte took off her jacket and I could see a crucifix around her neck, just above the V in her V-neck sweater. No, the sweater wasn't red. She put her arm around her husband. "I still can't believe it. I'm in shock, even though I haven't seen Parker in years, at least not close up."

Of course, she would say that if he attempted to re-ignite their affair, or perhaps have a quick indulgence for old times' sake, and she reacted with extreme prejudice. But that wouldn't work, would it, unless she just happened to be carrying a knife at the time?

"Were you at the Expo yesterday?" Mac wanted to know.

"No, I was here. We decided to keep the store open, even though there wouldn't be much business. The kids helped me. Hey, you guys are Sister Polly's friends, aren't you?"

"We have the honor to be among that legion," Mac assured her, meaning "yes."

"That sweet woman's counseling saved my life a few years ago, or at least my soul." *I'm not sure that's correct ranking of priorities, Rita.* "So, what are you two doing here so late?"

"Just talking to people who knew Parker," Daponte said before Mac could respond. "Trying to get a line on who would want to kill him."

He apparently didn't want his wife to know about the botched burglary, disclosing the motive for which would bring up the unpleasant topic of her long-ago infidelity.

Rita fingered her crucifix. "Well, some of the women who come in here are pretty vocal about not being fond of the way he draws all his females with enormous bazooms. But nobody would kill for that, would they?"

Mac shrugged his shoulders. "Who knows? Jefferson and I observed a confrontation the victim had three weeks ago with one such offended woman, Jessica Ballantine."

The name immediately registered with Rita Daponte. "Yeah, she definitely wasn't president of the Parker Williams fan club. But she's so buff she wouldn't need a knife to kill somebody—she could strangle him."

"Not every woman was so negative on Williams or his work," I said, thinking of Miranda Blackwood, Red Falcon fans, and presumably his first two wives, originally, as well as Rita herself.

"True enough," Daponte said. "Sandy Hollander buys every issue of Red Falcon and any other comic where the character appears."

"She was dressed the part on Saturday," I recalled. "Ms. Hollander told the cops she never met Williams. That's a little odd, now that I think about it. He wasn't a *bon vivant*, but a big fan of his work would have recognized him at some local go-to like Beans & Books or Bobbie McGee's, or even Lawrence's IGA. And wouldn't she have gushed and introduced herself?"

Daponte shrugged. "Sandy hasn't lived in Erin long—less than six months, I'd say. They moved here when her husband got a job as a project manager for the Altiora Corp. She works from home teaching French literature at one of those online universities."

Sacré bleu!

"Can you suggest any customers other than Ms. Ballantine who displayed a strong negativity toward Parker Williams's artwork?" Mac asked Rita.

The name of Helen DeVries, aka Red Raven, popped into my mind, but Rita declined Mac's invitation with a shake of her head. "I wouldn't want to do that. I mean, it's a pretty far-fetched murder motive when you think about it."

"SHE'S RIGHT, you know," I told Mac on the way home. "Granted, Williams's work was a bit over-the-top when it comes to female tops, but it's not like there are a lot of flat-chested women in comic books. I mean, think of Catwoman and Black Widow." I'd noticed those books in the store. It was hard not to. "So, if offensive art was the motive, why pick on Williams? There were probably half a dozen or more artists in the building that day equally guilty."

"You have unwittingly made an excellent argument in favor of Roscoe Feldman's theory, old boy."

"What? How so?"

"If the killer had her pick of victims, that would make a premeditated crime of opportunity all the easier. She simply killed the easiest prey."

"Oh."

"However," Mac sailed on, "that prescinds from the notion that one would kill out of a sense of aggrievement related to Mr. Williams's rather tasteless portrayal of women. Mrs. Daponte's characterization of that motive as 'far-fetched' is a reasonable one. While it is not impossible, and thus we cannot rule it out, it is not a high-priority theory."

"Well, that's just dandy! I get dragged away from hearth and home and into the dark on Valentine's Day, and for what? Our would-be burglars each have different theories and we don't have much faith in either one, especially Mary Lou's. As Daponte said, a murder at his Expo is the last thing he would want."

"I am not so sure of that," Mac said. "According to Assistant Chief Gibbons, Sunday attendance at the Expo was in no way diminished by the murder. Perhaps it was even boosted by it. And Mr. Daponte himself said that his store trade was quite brisk today."

"What are you saying?"

"I am saying that contrary to Mr. Daponte's assertion that the murder of a well-known artist at the Expo would have been the last thing he wanted for business reasons, that does not seem to have been the case. And, therefore, it is no contraindication of guilt."

"So, you think he's a hot suspect?"

"What I think, Jefferson, is that Mr. Daponte cannot be greatly mourning the death of Parker Williams."

Chapter Fifteen
Red-Eyed

TALL RAWLS LATER apologized for the big **WOMAN IN RED ELUSIVE** headline at the top of her Tuesday morning story in the *Observer*, which actually landed on the Cody front lawn this time instead of being AWOL. She thought it too sensational. The verbiage was picked up from the backfill near the end of the story, which mentioned the PublicEye attention to the case. Most of the piece was solid, though, accurately quoting Oscar on the status of the investigation ("ongoing . . . no higher priority . . . earliest stage . . . no arrests . . . no persons of interest") before going into a profile of Parker Williams that accented his long-distance marriage to a successful film actress before getting to the wild theories.

And then there was this gem of a quote from Sebastian McCabe: "I have every confidence in the Erin and St. Benignus police bringing the killer to justice."

"Does he really mean that?" GK asked me in an early morning phone call.

"By no means," I assured him. "He's on the case. He was reluctant at first—some kind of loss of confidence thing after that Bainbridge fiasco—but he's all in now."

"I'm counting on that."

Every media reference to the scene of the murder inevitably called it the SBU Towne Center. Although its connection to the university wasn't emphasized and probably didn't sink in for most readers, it stuck out like a hitchhiker's thumb to our president. Moreover, GK cannot have been pleased by our own student body's *The Spectator*, which came out on Tuesday with Cindy Weller's story about the murder across the top. But at least Weller quoted Dr. Susan Nelan on the new center's important role in "taking entrepreneurship out of the classroom and into the community." (I was rather proud of writing that line for Sue.)

On the positive side of the ledger, Popcorn and I spent half the morning strategizing a new SBU social media offensive with Riley St. Simon. Although she is also a dab hand at press releases, our magenta-haired intern specializes in Twitter and Instagram. (Magenta is not the same as red, by the way. Nor are puce or fuchsia, just for the record.)

"It's naïve to expect good news to drown out the bad," I told Riley, "but it puts it in perspective."

The eyes behind her big glasses told me I was preaching to the pig-tailed choir. "How about Instagram photos of our NAIA basketball champion Lady Dragons?"

"My favorite team!"

Together the three of us also came up with post-able images for Instagram from various academic disciplines as well as sports—business administration, fine and performing arts, engineering, criminal justice, and more. Thus engaged, my morning flew by.

After a healthful lunch at my desk, I wandered over to Mac's office in Herbert Hall. If I have given the impression in these chronicles that the McCabe quarters are a firetrap, with sagging bookshelves and books stacked everywhere, that is only because it is true. Fortunately, the "Thank You For Not Breathing While I Smoke" sign on his desk is but a sad (to him) reminder of an era long past. Even the ashtrays full of cigar butts and ashes of former days are gone. Mac ignored the campus-wide smoking ban for years but succumbed to Lesley Saylor-Mackie's personal appeal.

To my surprise and relief, he wasn't practicing a magic trick or playing his dreadful bagpipes upon my arrival. He was communing with his laptop.

"I told GK you were hard at work," was my entrance line. "Was I lying?"

"And good afternoon to you as well!" Mac boomed. "Having taught today's class"—even full professors have to do that occasionally—"I am reading the latest PublicEye posts by Bethany Lane on the Williams murder. Ms. Lane suggests that investigators search social media photos of the Expo and videos of the panels looking for an individual dressed as Red Falcon in the area of the murder scene. Alternatively, she posits that red jewelry, hats, shoes, dresses, pantsuits, scarves, or tattoos might be the intended clue."

"Anything but red hair works for me," I quipped. "Of course, Bethany doesn't know that Banfield and Gibbons have already been doing what she's calling for. In fact, at this point they must be red-eyed from looking for red. It's a regular red scare!"

Before Mac could laud that witticism, which I'm sure he would have, his cell rang. He immediately put the call on speakerphone.

"I hope Jeff is with you," Oscar said.

Why does everybody assume that I have nothing better to do than—

"As it happens, he just came into my office."

"Good. I wanted you supersleuths to know that my crack team has discovered the identity of Parker Williams's first two wives."

Whom Mac suggested as suspects about 24 hours ago!

Suppressing the thought—after all, we didn't hop on that angle either—I said instead, "Sarah-Jane Manders, the tattoo lady, was the second."

After what some old novels might have called a pregnant pause, Oscar responded with, "Uh, right. But the big reveal is wife numero uno—one Felicity Snow."

Frost-Pierson's lawyer!

"The devil you say!" was Mac's response.

"I thought that would get your attention." Oscar sounded smug. "Why wouldn't she tell us that unless she had something to hide?"

"Why not indeed!"

"So, Gibbons will interview both of the ex-widows, but with Banfield's help for the feminine touch." *She can deck them if they get rough.* "And the mayor suggested that it might be a good idea for you to go along."

"The mayor?" Mac repeated.

Reverend Fred Sutterlee had been elected to his second term as Erin's mayor the previous year. Though senior pastor of the Apostolic Holiness Church of the Holy Spirit, I sometimes think he regards the whole town as his congregation. In a good way.

"Yeah," Oscar confirmed. "It's budget time so I had to appear before city council's finance committee today to explain to those numbskulls that the price of gas is going through the roof of our cruisers and every other line item is going up as well. Anyway, the Reverend Mayor pulled me aside afterward to talk about the Williams murder. It was a follow-up to our phone conversation yesterday."

"And the mayor believes I might be helpful?"

"Well, he is a man of faith." *Good one, Oscar!* "I also had the feeling that the town fathers and mothers, the people who fund re-election campaigns, are a little edgy about seeing Erin in the national news combined with words like 'slain' and 'unsolved.'"

"I bow under the pressure," Mac said. *Throw me into that briar patch!* True, Mac had seemed genuinely loath to get involved at first, dogged by his missteps in the last case. But by Monday night he'd shed that like a snake leaving his old skin behind.

"What do the victim's two exes have to do with the color red?" I asked.

"Remember, the killer could have been wearing an identity-concealing costume," Mac said. "Perhaps Ms. Lane is on the right track about Red Falcon. And if not, there are many red-tinged characters in the superhero/supervillain sphere, from the Scarlet Witch to—"

"Red, schmed," Oscar said. "Red is going nowhere. We need to forget that and focus on facts. For instance, we know that Williams was stabbed in the heart with a very thin blade, more likely a knife than a sword."

"How many times?" Mac asked.

"Just once."

"Efficient," I commented.

"And delivered by someone either lacking in passion or in control of that passion," Mac said. "Interesting. What do you think happened to the knife?"

"Probably long gone. The Ohio River is handy for that."

We'd been down that road before.

"Perhaps. On the other hand, it is not inconceivable that the killer hid it somewhere that has eluded the best efforts of your capable officers."

I had a brainstorm, based on a speculation in a previous case.[13] It was wrong then, but maybe this time—

"What if it's hidden in Bobby Lumpkin's crutches!" I said. "They're hollow metal."

"It seems unlikely that a man on crutches would be able to stab Mr. Williams so effectively and then quickly leave the elevator," Mac objected.

Undeterred, I seized on the crutches for a possible motive. "Maybe Williams caused Lumpkin to have some horrible, permanently disabling accident which cried out for revenge. There's your motive!"

"Not quite," Oscar said. "Gibbons got curious about that, thinking maybe his temporary disability was faked. It turns out that Lumpkin hurt himself gaming. He got caught up in one of those virtual reality things and tripped over his sofa."

---

[13] Never mind which one.

Chapter Sixteen
Red Dragons

LATER, AT THE Beans & Books coffee house on Main Street, Mac said:

"Sherlock Holmes referred to the 'scarlet thread of murder running through the colourless skein of life.' An appropriate quote for this case, is it not?" The way he said it, I could practically hear the British spelling.

"So, are you thinking of scarlet as in Scarlett Featherstone? I thought she was off the radar—no known motive."

"Just musing, old boy."

"Well, cut it out."

Although I'd already eaten, I came along to watch Mac fuel up on caffeine and chicken salad while he mused before our appointments with the former Mrs. Williamses and law enforcement. He was there for the coffee beans, not for the used books for sale or for the art by female artists that had hung on the walls since the COVID-caused closing of the Looney Ladies Gallery.

I was just about to ask Mac where else I'd heard the word "scarlet" that day when a precise and familiar female voice said: "Good afternoon. How goes the sleuthing?"

While I turned around, Mac stood up in gentlemanly fashion to greet Amy Quong, the Gamble Bank honcho. A formidable woman, she once beat me at chess in six moves. And that was before she became the first non-Gamble to run the venerable financial institution.

"It goes slowly, Ms. Quong," Mac admitted.

Beneath her open camel's hair coat, I saw that her gray silk blouse was adorned with the same flower, or more probably the same kind of flower, she'd worn on Saturday.

"Is that a scarlet pimpernel?" I couldn't help asking, having that particular s-word on my mind.

"What? Oh, the flower. No, it's called a red camellia—very Asian. I wear it in sympathy with the people of my native city, Hong Kong, who have lost their freedoms under the communist yoke."

Aren't communists called 'reds'?!

"Would you care to join us?" Mac invited. We were sitting at a table with two empty seats.

"No, thank you. I am meeting—oh, here she is."

Coming in the front door, to my surprise, was a young black woman whom I quickly recognized as Triple M's friend Shalimar Burton, the media influencer that we'd met on Saturday. I wouldn't have put those two together, Burton and Quong. But after the usual greeting rituals, Quong explained the anomaly without my asking:

"Ms. Burton has a plan to create a mentoring program for returning citizens, individuals who were previously incarcerated and need help getting on a better path. We are discussing how the bank can help."

"Intriguing," Mac proclaimed the idea. He waved to the empty seats and the two women occupied them. Burton took off her jacket, revealing the same "superbabe" T-shirt we'd seen before with the caricature of her scantily clad self, pumping iron. The muscular arms beneath her short sleeves were decorated with tattoos of red dragons.

"You know about my social media work sending positive messages of empowerment for women, but did Sister Polly tell you about my 'life of crime'?" That last was said with a smile accompanied by air quotes.

A little of that had come up at the Super Bowl party.

"I gather that you were falsely convicted of what is technically called uttering bad checks," Mac said. "In other words, forgery."

She nodded. "Yeah, you got it. I was a dupe. My abusive boyfriend forged a check and had me cash it for him. I was convicted of a third-degree felony and sentenced to two years in prison and a fine of ten thousand dollars that I had no way to pay. The Innocence Project tracked down my scumbag ex and showed that he did the same thing in three other cities. They managed to convince the prosecutor that I got a raw deal, and he supported vacating my conviction."

Marvin Slade, said Sussex County prosecutor, just went up a notch in my estimation. It cannot have been easy for him to essentially undo the work of his office, especially since his conviction rate is what he campaigns on every four years. I didn't think he had it in him.

"I never went to prison, but I did spend some time in jail, which is where I met Sister Polly," Burton said. "We talked a lot. She became my friend, and that made me think. I was innocent, but even people who are guilty deserve a chance to start over. The problem is that a lot of them don't have the skills to get a job and stay on the straight and narrow. Even worse, they may not have any friends except the ones that got them into trouble to begin with. My Friends of Felons program would fix that."

"I think the name needs a little work," I volunteered. "'Felons' is a bit of a turnoff." Words are my business, and I made a mental note to come up with a better one for this worthy project.

Burton stopped talking while the server, who introduced herself as Ayesha, took the women's drink orders (coffee and Coke). When she departed, Mac said:

"You expressed very strong negative feelings about Mr. Williams on Saturday, both in person and on social media," Mac said, as if she didn't know that. "You told the police that he ill-treated a friend of yours whom you declined to name. Would you mind sharing that name with us, in complete confidence?"

Burton looked at Quong, then back at Mac. "Yes, I would mind. I don't want her pulled into this."

"She is already in it," Quong said. "If she is innocent, she has nothing to fear from Professor McCabe. He is thoroughly reliable. But if she killed her ex-husband, justice must be served."

"Ex-husband!" I didn't shout it. I hope.

Burton sighed. "Yeah. It's Sarah-Jane Manders. Williams totally destroyed her self-confidence, cheated on her with a woman named Daponte—after he cheated *with* her on his first wife. Why do people not understand that adultery is easier the second time around?"

Debatable, perhaps, but also plausible.

"How do you know Ms. Manders?" Mac asked.

She pointed to her arms. "There aren't prison tattoos! I had them done to remind me, to remind everybody, that women can slay the dragons in their lives, whatever they are."

"They're very red," I pointed out.

"And aren't they great?"

Mac was halfway through a dissertation on dragon legends around the world when Ayesha brought the drinks. The women started studying the menu.

"WELL, WHAT ARE you thinking?" I asked Mac about half an hour later as we walked down the sidewalk toward his gas-guzzler.

"Forgery," he said.

"Eh? Never mind her previous brush with the law. What about Burton as a suspect in the murder?"

Mac raised an eyebrow. "Surely nothing that Ms. Burton said pointed to her."

"Her arms did! She told the cops she never met Williams. Ergo, he wouldn't have known her name, but he would have known that her arms were red."

"And what do you posit as her motive?"

"Do I have to do all the work for you?" After some time, during which I couldn't think of a motive, I said: "And what about forgery, anyway?"

"Ms. Burton's reference to forgery reminded me that Oscar told us Red O'Connor was widely suspected of forging a valuable *Amazing Spider-Man* cover. Pair that with Rasputin Spargo's accusation that the *She-Wolf* cover on display at the Library & Museum of Popular Culture is inauthentic and that Parker Williams knew it. Perhaps Red O'Connor was the forger of that artwork. If Mr. Williams learned that and threatened to expose him, Mr. O'Connor might have killed to prevent that."

"We don't even know that Red forged the *Spider Man,* much less the *She-Wolf,*" I objected. "Oscar said he was the 'number one suspect,' but that doesn't mean he was guilty.

Maybe he was innocent—like Shalimar Burton!" I thought it rather neat the way I circled back to her, since it was her use of the word 'forgery' that set Mac's train of thought chugging down the track and possibly off the rails. "On the other hand, I have to admit that his name is Red."

"Valid points, Jefferson, both of them!" Mac said as he opened his car door. "Getting honest answers out of Mr. O'Connor could be difficult, given the fact that he may have committed a crime. For that reason, I hope to convince Oscar to let us speak to him alone after we have joined the assistant chiefs in their interviews with the two former Mrs. Williamses. I shall be particularly interested in what Felicity Snow has to say, in light of her lack of candor regarding her history as the first Mrs. Williams."

Chapter Seventeen
Red-Faced

"OKAY, I'M A little embarrassed that I didn't mention I was once married to the creep," Felicity Snow told us about fifteen minutes later. "But I was concentrating on representing my client and I didn't want to overcomplicate things. Besides, my ill-fated first marriage was long ago—twelve years. I was only twenty-one at the time and we divorced two and a half years later when I caught him fooling around with Sarah-Jane Manders. Parker was amazingly inept at adultery, though I suppose he got better with practice."

Gibbons, Banfield, Mac, and I were crammed into Snow's modest office where she was sharing space with a small law firm, Farleigh & Farleigh. She sat behind an unimpressive desk littered with *The Wall Street Journal* and assorted paperwork. Raven hair, blue eyes—I still couldn't shake the feeling that she reminded me of somebody. The diploma from the Salmon P. Chase College of Law on the wall behind her was only a couple of years old.

"Not bitter, are you?" Gibbons said.

She laughed. "Sorry about that. I was looking in my rear-view mirror for a while there and I didn't like what I saw. I hardly ever think—*thought*—of Parker, to tell you the truth. It didn't take me long to figure out I was best rid of him."

This had the ring of truth, not the words of a woman in denial. "Now I'm happily engaged to a wonderful man named Bob Cartwright. We used to teach together at Malcolm C. Cotton High. Sarah-Jane, on the other hand, never got over Parker, even though she was the one who called it quits."

Mac raised an eyebrow.

"How do you know that?" Banfield asked.

"Oh, we've been friends forever. In fact, that's how Parker met her. Sure, things got a little cool between Sarah-Jane and me when I found out what she and Parker were up to. And we didn't see each other much during the time they were married. But when Rita—Rita Ellison Daponte—broke up their marriage before she went slinking back to her husband, Sarah-Jane cried on my shoulder about divorcing Parker. She loved the weasel, even though she had too much self-respect to put up with what she could see was going to be a pattern of infidelity."

"Might her unrequited love have expressed itself in violence?" Mac asked.

Snow sat back. "You mean did she kill him, McCabe? No, of course not."

"Who do you think killed him?" Gibbons asked.

"Not my client, I can assure you again."

"Who then?" Banfield piled on.

"The woman in red, of course. Whoever that is."

"But you have no idea who that could be?" That was Mac.

She shrugged. "Maybe a jilted lover. I'm not a comic book fan and I wasn't at the Expo, so I can't help from that point of view."

"Where *were* you on Saturday?" I asked, dotting an i or crossing a t, depending on which figure of speech you prefer.

"I went shopping late in the morning at Findlay Market in Cincinnati, followed by a late lunch at a nearby delicatessen, and then a little shopping in the Over-the-Rhine neighborhood. I was alone, but I have a parking receipt that shows I was there until after four o'clock."

If she looked a little smug as she pulled the paper receipt out of her purse, I couldn't blame her. She held it out and Gibbons stood to take it.

The rest of us stood as well. We had reached that point.

"I congratulate your resilience, Ms. Snow," Mac said. "I am curious to know why you went into the law as a second career."

"It wasn't because I wanted to pile up all that student loan debt," she assured him. "Teaching wasn't fun anymore and I've always admired my aunt, Judge Kessler."

"Red Falcon!" I blurted out.

"Excuse me?" Snow said.

"Sorry. I've been trying to figure out who you remind me of. It's Red Falcon. You have her hair color and facial shape, never mind that she wears a mask while superheroing."

She grimaced. "I can't deny that Parker first drew the character while we were married and maybe based the image on me. But we're getting lost in the weeds here. You said you wanted to talk about Parker's murder. I hope that you're no longer interested in my client as a suspect."

"How did Mr. Frost-Pierson become your client?" Mac asked. "I presume that you have no particular expertise in the rather specialized field of law dealing with plagiarism."

"Strangely enough, that comes back to Sarah-Jane. She was following references to Parker on social media—not in a bad way, just keeping track of what he was up to. She's actually a fan of his work and of comic books in general. So, she saw the claims Gavin was making and mentioned it to me in a 'wow, you won't believe this crap' kind of way. I'm not overwhelmed with work, and I had no compunction about going after Parker, so I friended Gavin on Facebook and then FM'd him to offer my services."

This was a new take on ambulance chasing.

"What do you think would have happened if Mr. Williams had lived?"

"I suppose I can tell you it would have never gone to court; we didn't have any proof. But I was hoping that Parker's attorney—David Gunner—would convince Parker to spend a few thousand of his millions to pay Gavin to go away. I think I could have convinced Gavin to take the money and run, although his pride would have been against it. But that's irrelevant now. We'll have to deal with the heirs, who may have a counsel who wants to play hardball.

"Meanwhile, I gather from your non-answer that my client is still under a cloud of suspicion that won't go away until this murder is solved. It seems to me that you are going nowhere fast in accomplishing that, and that this interview has been a waste of time. So please do your job, gentlemen and lady. Find the woman in red."

Chapter Eighteen
Red Armed

SARAH-JANE MANDERS wore three-inch hoop earrings and had red arms sticking out of her T-shirt—tattoos of the Human Torch on the right one and a crimson-cloaked Dr. Strange on the left one. I hadn't seen the arms before, but I remembered her flowing pink hair amid the audience for the Scarlett Featherstone panel.

We visited Manders at her Artistic Ink Tattoo Studio on downtown's Spring Street, a business which seemed to be thriving after surviving the pandemic shutdown of 2020. She'd told Gibbons she could spare us 20 minutes between customers. She owned and operated the studio, but also had two tattooists working for her. Meeting with us in her back room, not up close with customers, she moved her white protective mask to her chin as she sat in a chair.

"Yeah, I was at the Expo," she told Gibbons in answer to his opening question. It's not unusual for police to ask questions to which they already know the answer as a check on the interviewee's veracity. That's why lying to a cop is never a good idea.

"I left here early—around lunch time—so I could catch the Scarlett Featherstone panel. I stayed until the announcement that Parker's panel was . . ."

She stopped, swallowed. Emotion or acting? I voted for the former.

Although pink was only one of many offbeat hair colors at the Expo, I'd noticed Manders (although I didn't know her) among the audience at the Featherstone panel. But since I'd then turned my attention to Scarlett Featherstone, and Winsome after that, I couldn't say for sure that Manders was still in that room when her ex-husband was killed.

"Were you with anyone?" Gibbons asked.

"No." She shook her head. "It's still hard to believe Parker's dead. Valentine's Day was the fifth anniversary of our divorce becoming final. How's that for an ironic date? The marriage lasted less than three years. I caught him getting it on with Al Daponte's wife, who I knew when she was Rita Ellison. I couldn't put up with Parker fooling around on me, never mind his protestations that it was 'just a fling.' What's *just* a fling? At least I got a good settlement out of Parker, unlike Felicity; that's how I started this place."

"You bore your former husband no animus, then?" Mac asked.

"Animus? I hated him, if that's what you mean." A wan expression stole over her face. "But I gotta say, I also loved him. I couldn't help myself. I've dated around a little since, but nothing serious. No other bad boy could quite match up."

"Have you had those tattoos long?" Banfield asked.

I knew what she was thinking: If Manders were the killer, and if the tattoos were long-standing, and if Williams saw the tatts—so many ifs!—Williams would have known who she was and wouldn't have had to leave such an obscure message.

"Ten years," Manders said. "Since I was twenty-one. The first thing Parker ever said to me was how cool they are."

"Do you know anyone who might have wanted to kill your former husband?" Gibbons asked.

She didn't have to think long. "Maybe that guy who says Parker stole his idea for Queen Bee."

"Do you think he did it?" I said, just to keep my hand in. "Stole the idea, I mean."

"I don't know. But knowing Parker, he might have put the idea aside and six months later convinced himself it was his own brainstorm."

"Some people might say that spouses, ex-spouses, and ex-lovers are good suspects," Banfield said, nicely distancing herself from the thought.

"Well, I know I didn't do it."

"That leaves one wife, one ex-wife, and at least one ex-lover but possibly more."

"Why are you trying to pull me into this?"

"Just getting your take, Ms. Manders. You obviously knew the dead man pretty well."

"All too well, maybe. But that doesn't mean I'm an authority on his other women. For what it's worth, though, I hear that Rita's been back with her husband more or less since I walked out on Parker. They have kids together and that's important to some people; it would be to me. So I guess they're making a go of it. And the only thing I know about Miranda Blackwood is that she's a damned good Red Falcon. Oh, and she's gorgeous."

"That leaves Ms. Snow," Mac observed.

Manders stood up, her twenty-minute window of opportunity about run out. "Don't waste your time on that idea. Parker is a dead letter to her. I guarantee you she didn't love him or hate him or think about him anymore. To her he was just a guy she married right out of college when she didn't know any better and before he hit it big."

"You seem pretty sure of that." Gibbons sounded skeptical.

"Felicity and I are good friends. We were friends before Parker and we're still friends after Parker, although there was a rough part there in the middle. If anything, we're closer now than we've ever been, thanks to bonding regularly over red wine and those gourmet meals she cooks up. She's getting married again this summer and I'm the bridesmaid. Believe me, Felicity Snow had no reason to kill Parker."

Chapter Nineteen

Red O'Connor

ONE OF THE worst parts about winter for me is that it's usually too cold to roll down the windows in protest when Mac lights up a cigar as he gets behind the wheel of the Macmobile. Which he did immediately after we left Artistic Ink and parted company with the forces of law and order.

"Well, Jefferson"—*puff, puff*—"what do you think of the quartet of Mr. Williams's former or present love interests? As suspects, I mean."

"Do you want them in chronological or alphabetical order?"

"Chronological. First, however, let us acknowledge the obvious: The only conceivable reasons for Mr. Williams not to give the name of his killer, rather than an obscure clue, are that (a) he did not know the attacker, or that (b) he did not recognize the person—most likely because of a costume or disguise. Now go ahead."

"So, you don't buy the idea that he was starting to write RED FALCON to point to Miranda Blackwood?"

"I do not. That alone does not rule her out as a suspect, however. Nor does the fact that Parker Williams would have recognized Ms. Manders by her tattoos, and therefore

they could not possibly have been the RED to which he referred, rule *her* out."

"No, that would be far too easy."

"They, like anyone else, could have been dressed in
concealing garments. Hell and damnation, Jefferson!" He
seemed a bit nettled. "In an exhibit hall full of costumes, anyone could have been wearing one—plus a protective mask.
Let us discard the dying message for the nonce."

"Right." *Whatever a nonce is.* "In chronological order,
then, we start with wife number one. Felicity Snow and her
gal pal, wife number two, agree that Snow has long since
moved on from Parker Williams and is happily engaged to
another guy. She doesn't seem to have profited by her ex's
death either financially or psychologically. In fact, she might
have made a few bucks if he'd lived and reached a settlement
for Gavin Frost-Pierson, from which she would have taken a
healthy slice as his lawyer."

Mac nodded. "She also has that alibi for Saturday, the
receipt for parking in Cincinnati at the time of the murder."

"The aforementioned wife number two, Sarah-Jane
Manders, also doesn't profit financially. She already got her
pound of flesh out of Williams when they divorced, and it
must have been substantial since it funded her tattoo parlor.
I'm sure she deserved it. But, even disregarding the money
angle, she had two motives for murder." I stopped—rather
dramatically, I thought.

"Expound, old boy."

This was kind of fun.

"The 'woman scorned' motive and the related 'if I
can't have him no one else can' motive. She admitted she

both hated and loved him. And she was at the Expo on Saturday."

Mac blew noxious smoke. "In a logical world, Ms. Manders might be expected to kill the paramour who broke up her marriage rather than the man she loved."

"For sure. In fact, both of the exes seem to have it in for Rita Daponte. But let's not get distracted by that. Even Sarah-Jane pointed out that Rita and her husband have been back on track, maritally speaking, for years. Also, she was at Graphic Images literally minding the store at the time of the murder."

"That brings us to the current Mrs. Williams."

"Wait a minute." I couldn't take it anymore. I rolled down the window and breathed fresh but freezing air for about thirty seconds, then rolled it back up.

"Okay," I said, "on to Miranda Blackwood. For reasons already discussed—namely, she didn't need his money and the text trail indicates she had his love or a reasonable facsimile—I don't think we'll see her on *The Next Twenty Most Horrifying Hollywood Murders*. She could probably prove she was at the Harridan at the time of the murder, if she needed to."

"Bravo, old boy! You scintillate this afternoon. Your analysis was clear and succinct."

"Yeah, it was a fast trip to nowhere."

"Now we can pick up that dropped stitch of Mr. Red O'Connor and the possibility that he killed Parker Williams to conceal his forgery of valuable comic book cover art. First, however, we have to find him."

Mac picked up his cell. I won't tell you who he called or describe in detail what happened next. If I did, Oscar would have a stroke and then fire somebody. Suffice it to say that through negotiation and wile, Mac obtained O'Connor's phone number from police sources speaking off the record. That was necessary because, as expected, the veteran artist had cleared out of town on Sunday.

O'Connor answered Mac's call with all the alacrity of an actor awaiting a call-back from an audition. The speaker was on for my benefit.

"Mr. O'Connor? Sebastian McCabe here!"

"Who?"

This won't be easy.

"We met on Saturday. I was part of your interview with the Erin and St. Benignus police, both of which I assist in an advisory capacity."

"I still don't know—oh, wait. Were you the big fat guy with the beard who talked a lot?"

"That is a reasonably accurate description." *I'd call it dead-on.*

"What do you want?"

"I would like to arrange a Zoom call"—Mac's idea was that seeing the guy's face would give him a better read on whether he was lying—"to speak with you about your art forgery and how it might relate to the murder of Parker Williams."

We didn't know for sure whether O'Connor had forged anything, but O'Connor didn't know that.

"I have nothing to say to you."

The phone went dead.

"That was quick," I observed.

"Not totally unexpected," Mac grunted. He touched his phone for a recall. Surprisingly, O'Connor answered instead of letting it go to voicemail.

"I told you—"

"Would you rather talk to the police?"

"I thought you were the police."

"I am an unpaid consultant, and therefore a free agent. If I am convinced that you had nothing to do with Mr. Williams's murder, other crimes that you have committed are of no interest to me and knowledge of them will not be shared with the authorities."

It was something of a shot in the dark, that reference to "other crimes," but O'Connor's response showed that it was an accurate shot nonetheless.

"How the hell do I know that you'll honor that deal, McCabe?"

"You have only my word. You also have my word that if you do not speak with me, I will do my best to assure that you receive a call from Erin Assistant Chief L. Jack Gibbons and it will not be as friendly a conversation as this one."

After a little more dancing, O'Connor agreed to take part in a Zoom call at 4 P.M. He provided an email address for the invitation. After putting in a guest appearance in my own office for a couple of hours, I showed up at Mac's in Herbert Hall to gather around his laptop several minutes before the appointed hour.

"Read this," Mac instructed me, angling the laptop my way. "This" was a sad story about Red O'Connor from an online comic book fanzine. It related that his career crashed in the mid-1980s, toward the end of the Bronze Age of comic books, highlighted (or lowlighted) by him being institutionalized. The inference was that nonprescription pharmaceuticals were involved in his downward spiral.

Just as I finished the story, headlined "A Fallen Star," Mac made the appropriate cursor clicks and O'Connor's face filled the laptop screen. Close-up, the bags under his watery blue eyes looked like they were packed for a long trip. His wispy hair seemed to have more gray and less red than the previous week. He sat in a sparsely furnished room with what looked like cheap wood paneling decorated with cover illustrations for comic books—Gold, Silver, or Bronze Age, I couldn't tell you.

"Ah, here we are," Mac said.

"The pleasure is all yours." I bet O'Connor had that line ready to go.

"No doubt. I will be brief and direct, Mr. O'Connor. Chief Hummel is aware that last year you were widely suspected of forging a Steve Ditko *Amazing Spider-Man* cover that initially sold for a great deal of money until it was revealed as spurious."

"It must have been a very good forgery." O'Connor couldn't keep the smugness out of his voice, which was amplified by the look on his face. "But I'm sure your small-town police chief also told you the perpetrator was never identified."

Mac laid it on with a trowel: "I would hardly expect the artistic genius behind that impressive work to admit it in so many words. I only wish that he were here to take a bow."

With a Mona Lisa smile on his face, O'Connor leaned forward slightly in his chair, then back again. *Point made!*

"Okay, I'll bite," he said. "What does somebody's masterful copy of Ditko at his best have to do with the price of tea in China?" *Which is going up, along with the price of everything else.* "I thought you were poking into the murder of Parker Williams. What's the connection?"

"Forgery," Mac said. "A man named Rasputin Spargo contends that a *She-Wolf* cover on display at the Library & Museum of Popular Culture is a copy, and that Parker Williams knew it because he owned the original in his private collection. If Mr. Williams did indeed know that, he might also know who forged it—knowledge that the forger could quite conceivably kill to suppress."

"Horse hockey!" He really said that.

"You demur? I am surprised. Surely you cannot deny that concealment of a crime is a strong motive. Or are you denying the initial crime? We have established that you are a master forger, sir. And surely the imitation *She-Wolf* cover must have been masterful to fool Mr. Post at the Library & Museum."

"I'm not admitting anything," O'Connor said. Then he proceeded to shovel dirt on his own grave. Never underestimate the self-destructive power of ego. "But if I did do it, that wouldn't have given me any reason to kill Williams because he wouldn't have known that was my work. And by the way, I bet the person who did draw the cover only executed a commission for a client and had nothing to do with selling it to that museum in Brattleboro."

"And who might that client have been?" I asked, both keeping up the farce and beating Mac to the question.

The forger's mouth quirked into a funny smile. He was enjoying this despite himself. "Try Rasputin Spargo."

A McCabe eyebrow shot up. "By thunder, I find that highly credible, Mr. O'Connor! I never believed that he was an innocent receiver of stolen goods in the case of the Elbridge Gerry University Library thefts. Therefore, his dishonesty is no surprise to me." He thought a moment. "By selling to Graham Bentley Post—through a third party—what would later prove to be a forgery, Mr. Spargo intended to ruin the reputation of the Library so that collectors would no longer find it a natural recipient for their largesse."

"Yeah, what you said. I mean, theoretically."

"And if Parker Williams somehow ferreted out the scheme—"

"That would give Spargo a murder motive at least as great as that of the forger, or even greater because the scheme was his," I jumped in. "We ought to talk to Spargo again."

"I happen to know that he's still in your burg," O'Connor said. "He told me he was going to get some of Parker's art out of the widow or die trying."

"Another motive! Get from the widow what he'd never be able to get from Williams during his lifetime."

"Do you know where Mr. Spargo is staying in Erin?" Mac asked.

"He mentioned it in passing, but I forget the name. Some fancy-ass hotel downtown."

"It has to be either the Winfield or the Harridan," I said.

"Winfield sounds right."

"I'm not surprised. He wouldn't be holed up at Motel 6, what with his fancy vest and walking stick."

"Walking stick!" Mac repeated. "Why did I not think of that before?"

"What?" O'Connor leaned forward.

"You have been very helpful, Mr. O'Connor, and I thank you. Have a pleasant evening."

"But—" was all O'Connor could get out before Mac ended the Zoom call and turned to me.

"Parker Williams was killed by a thin blade. The sort of walking stick that Rasputin Spargo carries sometimes conceals such a blade within. We even saw him brandishing it as though it were a sword at the lobby of the Harridan when we called on Miranda Blackwood."

SOMETIMES YOU GET lucky. The bar of the Winfield, called Malarkey's Pub (separate from the more formal Mimosa restaurant), is right off the lobby—where we found Rasputin Spargo. I spotted him by his sizable Vandyke. He'd shed the suit coat but still wore a paisley vest, and his stick was propped up against the bar.

"Hello, gentlemen," he said as we occupied bar stools on either side of him. He wasn't glassy-eyed, but he spoke very carefully. He had a double of something brown in his hand, and I didn't think it was his first. "Buy you a drink?"

"Too early," I said.

"Yes, thank you," Mac responded at the same time. He ordered a Queen City Stout.

"Have you found Parker's murderer?" Spargo asked.

"We progress in that direction," Mac said.

"In other words, no."

"We have, however, found out some interesting and perhaps significant things about various personalities involved in our investigation."

Tired of this foreplay, I expounded for Spargo: "Such as the fact that you hired Red O'Connor to forge a painting of a comic book cover so that you could dupe Graham Bentley Post into buying it for his museum, thereby ruining the museum's reputation and giving you a better shot at getting your hands on some goodies that might otherwise wind up there." I turned to Mac. "Did I miss anything?"

"Only that if Parker Williams knew this, it would be a reason for Mr. Spargo to cause him to shed his mortal coil."

"In other words," I told Spargo, "a motive for murder."

"Eh?"

Spargo emitted a hollow laugh, about as phony as a politician's promise. "That's pure who-shot-John."

"Eh?"

"Fiction. Like what you write, McCabe. I've been reading your book *Now You See It* on Kindle. When it comes to magician sleuths, I prefer the Great Merlini to your Damon Devlin."

One shouldn't argue tastes, and Mac didn't. "Which part of the scenario we have outlined do you deny?"

Spargo gave what he probably thought was a canny look. "Without commenting on any other part, I certainly had nothing to do with Parker Williams's death." *In other words, I paid for the forgery, but I'm not going to say that.* "In fact, I regret it very much. I was counting on Parker to go public with the fact that he owns the original of that *She-Wolf* forgery up in Vermont."

That sounded pretty good to me, until Mac raised the other potential motive.

"I understand that you are attempting to buy some of Mr. Williams's collection from his widow."

That elicited a nod from Spargo, after a bracing gulp of the brown liquid. "I was, but no joy. Not yet. Miranda Blackwood wants to have an independent appraiser put a price on everything first. So, I'm leaving town tomorrow. But that doesn't mean I'm giving up. I never give up."

"Was the genuine *She-Wolf* cover one of the items you attempted to buy?"

"I don't see how that's any of your business."

"We can ask Ms. Blackwood."

The bartender set Mac's stout in front of him with a smile and efficiently departed.

"All right, yeah, I want to buy it," Spargo admitted in the bartender's wake. "That's what collectors do."

"Granted, Mr. Spargo. I have that affliction myself with regard to books. I would note, however, that if you had succeeded in buying it, you would no longer need Parker Williams. With the original in your own hands, and a clear provenance to it, you could have used it to prove the inauthenticity of the one at the Library & Museum. So, Mr. Williams remaining alive was not necessary to your plan."

Spargo smiled. "But I didn't succeed in buying it."

"Not yet." Mac took a healthy gulp of his stout. "However, by your own admission, you never give up."

"I didn't kill Parker Williams. I don't know who killed Parker Williams or why. Those are categorical statements. As for the rest, let's just say that I'm pretty sure that if somebody paid to have that *She-Wolf* copied there was no personal check involved, so good luck proving it."

"May I look at your walking stick?"

Spargo regarded Mac as if counting the number of his heads. "What?"

"I affect one myself on occasion, though hardly as attractive as yours." Without asking permission again, he picked up the stick in his right hand and made a show of examining the brass eagle head. "Those diamonds that form the eagle's eyes are genuine, are they not?"

"Sure. I don't go in for fakery."

With a sudden move, Mac yanked on the head of the stick with his left hand. Nothing happened.

"What the hell are you doing, McCabe?"

Mac handed the stick back to Spargo, a grim look on his hirsute face. "I thought perhaps a sword was concealed inside. Such implements are not rare."

"Oh, yeah? Satisfied?"

"Not at all," Mac grunted. "I am, however, convinced of my own folly."

He finished the Queen City Stout to the soundtrack of Spargo's laughter.

Chapter Twenty

Red Meat

"DID IT EVER occur to you that Bruce Wayne had the first man cave, only he called it a batcave?" I asked Mac that evening after dinner at our respective haciendas.

"No, Jefferson, I am forced to give you full credit for that insight."

"You're welcome."

We were in the room at Mac's house on Half Moon Street that he insists on calling a study but has all the accoutrements of a man cave: leather chairs, fireplace, a flat-screen TV over the small wet bar with beer and Coke taps, books on all four walls, and the handsome walnut computer desk where Mac writes his own tomes of mystery fiction and obscure literary scholarship. Our agenda was to take a 10,000-foot view of suspects in the Williams murder. Lynda was on a girls' night out with Triple M and Johanna, while Rebecca and her sister Amanda were watching the Cody offspring.

I drew myself a Caffeine-Free Diet Coke from a tap while Mac did likewise with a Flying Pig porter. I had to keep my head clear.

"Rebecca seems okay," I commented.

"Indeed, she does. And I pray that appearances are not deceiving in this instance. I suppose her discovering the body would have been even more traumatic had she known the victim."

A random thought ricocheted through my brain and out of my mouth: "Are you sure she didn't?"

"Quite sure. Kate asked her, thinking that it might be better for the question to come from the maternal parent." Only Sebastian McCabe would say "maternal parent," but I caught the drift: Females tell their mothers things they don't tell their fathers. Or so fathers suspect.

Mac moved on. "We have been concentrating on motive since means and opportunity are not very helpful in this case, given that anyone might have concealed a knife on his or her person—"

"In a walking stick, for instance."

"—and then either discarded it someplace at the Towne Center where we have not yet found it, or left the facility with the weapon before the murder was discovered. Unfortunately, we cannot have a complete list of all the Expo participants near the murder scene on Saturday because some undoubtedly departed before Oscar's troops metaphorically sealed the doors. And so, to motive. I have been mentally reviewing the motives of all the killers we encountered in previous investigations with the idea of creating a chart."

Charts are red meat to my brother-in-law. He sat at his desk, opened his laptop, and played over the keys as he held forth in full McCabe lecture mode.

"Paradoxically, the first murder motive that leaps to mind here is love. Perhaps there is symbolic significance to the fact that the victim was stabbed in the heart. You mentioned what you called the 'woman scorned' motive and the 'if I can't have him no one else can' motive in conjunction with Sarah-Jane Manders. Another love-related motive would be the elimination of Parker Williams as a love rival."

"In which case, the killer would be male."

"Not necessarily, old boy! Although, statistically speaking, I think that is more likely. And we have already posited that the killer could be a man dressed as a woman or a man with a woman."

"The second classic motive is money," I nudged.

Mac nodded. "Perhaps it would be better to say financial gain, sometimes in a way that is not obvious."

"Such as?"

He cited the Hunter Davenport murder, in which the motive was distinctly unobvious.[14] "Or imagine a situation in which Party A kills Party B knowing that Party C will inherit – and Party A is the heir of Party C."

Got that?

"Enough with the alphabet soup," I said. "What have you got besides love and money? Or financial gain, if you want to call it that."

"Retribution—the motive of the first Sherlock Holmes story, *A Study in Scarlet*, which I quoted to you at lunch. We are having our very own study in scarlet, are we not?"

"I knew you'd say that eventually."

"At any rate, the murder could be a matter of revenge for an offense to the killer or to someone the killer loves.

"The fourth and final category of motives we have encountered before is self-preservation, the elimination of a perceived threat from the victim. This could be the murder of a blackmailer or anyone else who has knowledge that is

---

[14] See *Death Masque* (MX Publishing, 2018).

dangerous to the killer. It is often the spark that sets off the second murder in a case."

"We do seem to have a lot of those."

"I believe that exhausts the list of likely motives, old boy."

"Not quite," I pushed back. "You forgot about plain old hatred." While Mac raised an eyebrow and quaffed his beer, I expounded. "In real life, unlike in your books, people kill each other for road rage or because they're pissed off about something."

"That is beyond dispute. If the motive is that flimsy, however, it is useless to us as a means to uncover the culprit. Let us agree that any animus of which we are aware can be shoehorned into the category of 'retribution.'"

"Call it payback and we have a deal," I said, just to assert myself.

The McCabe fingers went to work and produced this chart on his computer screen:

MURDER MOTIVES

Love	Financial Gain	Payback	Self-Preser-vation

"Now all that remains is to attach names to these categories of motives," Mac said, as though that were easy.

"Well, we know we can't put Williams's wives under the heading of 'financial gain,'" I said.

"There is at least no *known* financial gain for the first two spouses. That is not true of Ms. Blackwood. Under the laws of the state of Ohio, Parker Williams could not have disinherited her even if he wished. And he did not wish. I asked Oscar and he confirmed for me that Mr. Williams's attorney, James Bridges, said that the deceased's current wife gets the bulk of his estate after a few charitable bequests."

"I already pointed out this afternoon that Miranda Blackwood, being a Hollywood A-lister, certainly didn't need Williams's money."

"And I did not object, because that statement was accurate. However, needing and wanting are two different things. Her name goes on the chart."

"Okay; it's your chart. Let's stick with suspects and see if there's a category each one fits into. Next up: Sarah-Jane Manders. She admitted she both hated and loved the victim, so I think she's on the chart in the 'love' motive category for the aforementioned reasons. That 'woman scorned' thing could put her under Payback, but let's consider that part of Love for simplicity."

"Very well." Mac typed her name into his chart. "On to Mrs. Daponte. We have already noted that by all accounts she was no longer smitten with her one-time paramour. Quite the contrary. She also has no financial motive. Retribution for what her liaison with Mr. Williams did to her marriage? Unlikely, given that her marriage endures. If there is a self-preservation motive for her, I do not see it. What other women shall we consider before we move on to the men?"

I considered. "Well, we know that Shalimar Burton had a mad-on against Williams because of the way he treated Manders, but she also has an alibi in the form of Alexandra Hale, who was a friend of Williams. Also, I like her."

"We can consider alibis later. Right now, let us concentrate on motives."

"All right. Helen DeVries—who was undoubtedly a woman in red while dressed as Red Raven—was among those who didn't appreciate Williams's, shall we say, highly three-dimensional women. File her under Payback along with Burton, even though I'm skeptical. And by the way, Jessica Ballantine—Roscoe's choice for the killer—was another such critic, as we saw for ourselves at that Poisoned Pens meeting."

"And I shall long remember it!"

"So, Ballantine goes in the same column. Sandy Hollander, just for variety, was a mega-fan who, theoretically, might have had some romantic dream involving Williams that went catawampus when she actually met him. That would require her to just happen to find a knife handy at the time, but if we're not considering alibis at this point then we shouldn't consider means and opportunity."

"Very well. All of those women are on the chart. Can we rule out the actors? You will recall that Aurelia Banfield said there was no known connection between Parker Williams and either Tamsin Crowley or Llewellyn Chase. I confirmed with Aurelia this afternoon that she conducted an internet search of the sort that would turn up any gossip, of which there was none."

"Speaking of gossip—and thanks for the segue—Miranda Blackwood and Winsome Lerouge are equally adamant that tabloid reports of something between Williams and Winsome are what Red O'Connor would call horse hockey. On that basis, neither of them would have a love motive. Neither would Scarlett Featherstone, who is either having a major love affair with the person in her mirror or she's a better actress than I think."

"I agree with all points as stated, Jefferson. Well done and well said! Let us turn our attention to the men, starting with Red O'Connor."

"I think I saw his picture in the dictionary under the word 'dodgy.' He says there's no way Williams could have known he forged the *She-Wolf* cover and blown the whistle on him, but we don't know that. Maybe Williams strongly suspected the truth and confronted O'Connor, who had a knife that found its way into Williams's heart during the course of an argument."

"Finally, a suspect with a self-preservation motive!"

"And Rasputin Spargo is the second name in that column, under exactly the same scenario," I said. "To wit: Williams could have known or strongly suspected that the forgery of an artwork he owned was being used to take down Post's Museum of Popular Culture. It doesn't take much imagination to see Williams resenting the way he was being played, which means he wasn't going to be quiet about it."

"That is not impossible."

"Then there's that Gavin Frost-Pierson."

"I sense a certain negative bias on your part regarding him, Jefferson."

"Nonsense. I actually feel sorry for the guy, especially if he really did create a character that Williams swiped. His career hasn't exactly set the world on fire." I waved that away with my Coke-bearing right hand. "Anyway, that has no bearing on the fact that he apparently was pounding his head against a brick wall and getting nowhere fast in his attempt to wring some money and—I assume—recognition out of the late Parker Williams. And frustration can lead to violence."

Mac opened his mouth, but I cut him off.

"I know that even though he was wearing a red baseball cap Williams didn't need to identify him by color since he knew him by name, and I know there's no obvious woman to help him, since lawyers generally don't do that as part of their service, but we're just talking motives here."

"I was about to say that I will put Mr. Frost-Pierson's name in what you insisted I call the 'Payback' column. Anyone else?"

"For an outside-the-box idea, how about Kyle Rufus, Miranda Blackwood's personal assistant?" *Something about that name* . . . "Maybe he had romantic designs on his boss."

"You posit elimination of a love rival as the motive." The broad McCabe phiz looked skeptical. "You will recall, of course, that the text record indicates no marital discord in the Williams-Blackwood relationship."

"That's no objection. If their marriage was solid as a rock, that would give Rufus a perfect motive for killing the husband. Hollywood types occasionally marry cameramen or whatnot, so maybe he had a fantasy along those lines."

"Though doubtful, I will add Mr. Rufus to the 'Love' column."

"Wait a minute!" I said. "That name—Rufus! It's been bothering me, and I just remembered why. Doesn't that mean red, or reddish, or red-headed in Latin?"

"Indeed it does, old boy! You surprise me. How did you know?"

DAN ANDRIACCO

"It was the answer to a clue in one of Lynda's cross-word puzzles a few weeks ago."

"The question of why Parker Williams would write 'red' rather than 'Rufus' is an even bigger puzzle. It strains credulity." But Mac typed in the name on his chart anyway.

"I believe that covers all serious suspects on the basis of motive. Bobby Lumpkin was on Assistant Chief Banfield's list because he wore a red jacket, but if there is any motive for him it is not apparent. Here is how we stand:"

He turned the laptop to show me the chart.

MURDER MOTIVES

Love	Financial Gain	Payback	Self-Preservation
S.-J. Manders S. Hollander K. Rufus	M. Blackwood	S. Burton H. DeVries J. Ballantine Frost-Pierson	R. O'Connor R. Spargo

"I would note that several of these individuals are known to be dishonest," Mac said. "Sarah-Jane Manders was involved with a married man. That is often colloquially referred to as 'cheating.' Red O'Connor committed forgery, at the behest of Mr. Spargo, a receiver of stolen goods. Even your friend Mr. Frost-Pierson falsified threats against his own life." He sighed.

Forestalling the inevitable McCabe reflection on the consequences of original sin, I said:

"There's a problem with this neat listing of motives, Mac."

He raised an eyebrow. "Have we missed one?"

"Not that I know of. But maybe the killer had no motive. Maybe Parker Williams was murdered by a complete fruit loop who didn't even know him."

Chapter Twenty-One
Red Falcon

"Nine-one-one. What is your emergency?"
"Murder! There's been a murder! I found the body."
"Where are you, sir?"
"2852 Rachel's Way. It's a private house. She's dead. I can't believe she's dead."
"Who's dead, sir?"

I DIDN'T KNOW about the 911 call until later, of course. On the morning of Wednesday, February 16, I was working out at Nouveau Shape. Although Lynda had been getting in daily gym time since the end of the COVID shutdown—and it showed!—I'd found it hard to get back into the habit. But there I was, a man with a mission—which wasn't to get in shape. I wanted to ask personal trainer Jessica Ballantine, listed on Mac's chart under "Payback," a few subtle questions about her and the late Parker Williams.

"I was like, 'I can't believe this' when I heard he was dead," she said in response to my opening salvo, which was of the "isn't it awful about" variety. "I've never known a murder victim. I was freaked out."

"But not unhappy," I suggested.

"What do you mean?" Her face, unseasonably tan against her short dark hair, was all innocence. Somehow in her shorts and T-shirt she looked even younger than she had at the Poisoned Pens meeting.

"Well, you were pretty negative about him and his work the last time I saw you." I tried to make it sound like a throwaway comment. "You know, the Poisoned Pens."

She winced. "I try not to remember that. Look, I completely overreacted that night because I was a little down on the male of the species at the time. I'd just broken up with my boyfriend—his idea—and I'd practically had to use martial arts that afternoon to fend off the manager here, who's a complete asswipe."

"Sean?"

She smiled. "Ex-manager, I should say. He was fired last week for sexual harassment. I can take partial credit."

What would Sebastian McCabe say to that?

"Brava," I told her. "Hey, you're a comic book fan, aren't you?"

She nodded. "Yeah, sure, that's how I even knew about Parker Williams and his big-busted babes. I'm more of a Harley Quinn fan, but I knew his reputation."

This sounded like a pre-emptive strike, Ballantine signaling before I even asked that she had no personal motive to poke a hole in Williams's fickle heart—which I wouldn't have, anyway. because I wasn't thinking that way at all.

"So, did you go to the Expo over the weekend?"

"I couldn't. I just flew back from Cancun on Monday. Where do you think I got this tan?"

Ballantine would have been foolish to lie about that, given that Oscar could check the airline records. Besides, the tan was convincing. She'd been somewhere recently, even if it was only under a sunlamp. But I wouldn't say that I slunk out of Nouveau Shape after my session on the elliptical machine, head bowed in defeat. After all, eliminating a suspect—even a minor one—is progress of a sort. Not that I especially felt like crowing about it when I saw that Mac was calling my cell just as I left the gym.

"Cody & McCabe, private eyes," I answered. "Riddles unraveled, enigmas—"

"There's been another murder," Mac said. "Meet me at 2852 Rachel's Way. Oscar is on his way."

"Isn't that Parker Williams's house?"

"It was. Miranda Blackwood would have inherited it had she not been killed there last night."

RACHEL'S WAY IS about a ten-minute drive from the gym in my aging New Beetle. Before hopping into my faithful steed, I called GK to loop him in. After some internal debate, I settled on the bad news–good news approach: "Miranda Blackwood has been murdered. Not on campus." His response was prayerful: "Great God have mercy!"

Officer Bertsch met me outside and ushered me through the crime scene tape. EMTs were carrying out the draped body of the beautiful Miranda Blackwood. Not seeing Arly Eppensteiner, I figured the coroner had been and gone or was otherwise occupied that morning.

Inside, the huge artist's studio on the lower level was as I remembered it from our interview with Williams during the investigation almost five years earlier—except for the disarray. File cabinet drawers were open and some papers with sketches were on the floor. But the studio was still filled with statues of superheroes and framed art of what I assumed to be original covers of Superman, Batman, Captain America, Iron Man—*and She-Wolf!* The last was a wild-eyed woman in a red halter top and a short red skirt, knife in hand.

Most of this I noticed only later, though, along with cigarette butts, empty Red Bull cans, a turntable, and shelves of vinyl records. What caught my eye first was the dried blood on the floor and on the statue of Red Falcon, which lay near where chalk marks indicated the bludgeoned body of Miranda Blackwood had been found. Oscar's officers were taking photos and dusting for prints. Banfield didn't get a share of this one, the home not being an extension of SBU.

Kyle Rufus, the dead woman's personal *(how personal?)* assistant sat slumped in a chair, his massive arms on his legs and a paper cup of coffee in his left hand.

". . . which wasn't like her," he was telling Mac, Oscar, and Gibbons in a controlled voice. Not unemotional; controlled. "She always answered my texts right away. But the last message I had from her was at seven o'clock last night saying she was coming over here."

"The coroner's early guess is that she died before midnight," Gibbons informed him.

Rufus shook his head. "I had a bad feeling about her not answering me and I didn't sleep well."

"You have separate hotel rooms?" Mac asked.

"What? Of course, we do. Did. But adjoining. I was security as well as her PA."

It would be only a slight exaggeration to say that the presidential suite of the Harridan is so big he could be holed up in the south wing and they'd never see each other, but Mac let that pass.

"So, you tried again this morning," Oscar prodded.

"Right. I texted, no answer. I called, and it went to voicemail. So, I Ubered over here. I rang the door and there was no answer. I rang it again, still no answer. So, I tried the door. It was unlocked, so I went in. I called her name several times, then I started walking around. I was afraid she was sick, maybe even unconscious. Nothing on the main floor, so I came down here. That's when I found her and called nine-one-one." He chugged coffee as if it were whiskey. "Last night, when she texted that she was coming over I texted back that I should go with her, but she said she wanted to be by herself. She didn't explain why. Maybe she had something to do, or she just wanted to be here with what's left of her husband, all his stuff; I dunno. That's not the sort of thing she would tell me. I wouldn't expect her to. I was a hired hand. A very well-paid hired hand for almost two years now, but a hired hand."

That sounded legit, but Rufus could have been a budding actor, for all I knew. And I didn't forget that his name means red, or reddish, or red-haired, despite Mac's observation that it would have been just as easy for Williams to write his name as the word RED.

"You texted a lot with Ms. Blackwood?" Oscar asked.

"Sure. All the time."

The Chief held up a mobile in a plastic bag. "The texts that you are talking about will be on here, right?"

"Sure." Rufus set down the coffee cup and pulled his own phone out of his left pants pocket. "Also in here. Check it out if you want." It was an offer, not a challenge, but Rufus knew what was going on: Oscar's army (probably Gibbons) would be following the text trail in search of anything murder-relevant.

"That won't be necessary. We'll be checking out Ms. Blackwood's phone anyway. By the way, when did you get to town?"

"I flew in on Sunday at Miranda's request."

The day after the murder, and very checkable through the airline.

"You mentioned security," Mac reminded Rufus. "Would it be accurate to say you were, in common terms, Ms. Blackwood's bodyguard?"

"That's a fair enough description."

"Was she under some particular threat?"

"No more than usual for any public personality. That's why she had me, and the guy before me, doing double duty instead of a full-time bodyguard. She was somewhat concerned about nuts, though, because she lived alone with her son. That's why she installed me in her guest house. It's part of my compensation." He shook his head. "I don't know what's going to happen to Elias, the poor kid."

"What about his father?" I asked, hoping for an inside scoop.

"I don't know who that is. Nobody knows, except maybe Harry Schwartz—he's her attorney, a fairly big name in the Hollywood legal world. I'd better call him as soon as you let me go. He'll probably want to come out here to deal with this hands-on."

Oh, good—another cook to spoil the soup.

Oscar looked at Mac and me, his face a question mark. Since we didn't say anything, he told Rufus: "You can go. I just have one more question. Ms. Blackwood must have let her killer in, seeing as how there was no break-in. So, it was probably somebody she knew. Do you have any idea who that might have been?"

The PA-cum-bodyguard shook his sandy head. "I haven't a clue, Chief."

We don't need a clue anyway; we need a solution.

OSCAR LOOKED AROUND the studio almost wistfully after Rufus had gone, escorted out by Gibbons. "It would be awfully nice if this mess is just what it looks like—an intruder looking for something gets interrupted by the owner-in-waiting and bashes her over the head with a handy statue."

"Which just happens to be a statue of the character she brought to life in the movies," I supplied.

"Coincidences are permissible in real life," Mac said, "though not in fiction. However, that scenario does upend your own assumption that Ms. Blackwood let her killer in, Oscar."

The Chief shrugged. "Not a problem. Williams must have left a key under the mat or in some other obvious place. Otherwise-smart people do that all the time. What do you think the killer was looking for?"

He was asking Mac, but I answered: "How about proof that Gavin Frost-Pierson created the character that became known as Queen Bee?"

"Excellent, Jefferson!" Mac said. "And yet . . . presuming that you posit Mr. Frost-Pierson as the individual involved, how could he use such evidence? If he sent Mr. Williams an original drawing and a scenario, as he asserts, how could he bring those items forward and yet prove that they were in Mr. Williams's possession?"

I was ahead of him for a change. "He wouldn't have to. Once he knew that they were here, there's probably some legal mechanism to have the place searched—maybe part of that thing called 'discovery.'" And then another thought hit me: "Maybe he wasn't looking for proof but was planting it!" That actually made sense. The Cody brain was on fire!

Mac raised an eyebrow. "By thunder! You are developing a devious mind, old boy."

"Thanks."

"To answer Oscar's question, there is no real way to know what the killer was looking for if he or she found it and removed it—unless, of course, there is an inventory somewhere."

"I suppose we should look around and see what we can see or not see," Oscar suggested. He may have been kidding, but Mac took the bull by the horns and steered it.

"Let me call your attention to that cover of the first *She-Wolf* comic book framed on the far wall." he said. That to which he pointed was 10x15 inches, not counting the frame. Most of the artwork surrounding it was the same size, although some was larger and apparently older. "That is no doubt the original of which a copy is on display at the Library & Museum of Popular Culture. That is worth noting as supporting that part of Rasputin Spargo's story."

"Assuming, of course, that it's not the other way around, with this one a forgery and the other the original," I volleyed back.

"No one has suggested that."

"I just did." Not that I believed it, but it was fun playing with Mac's head.

"Noted," he said. "I see that Mr. Williams was at work on a new issue of *Red Falcon*. Perhaps the storyline is revealing. It is even conceivable that he was killed to prevent him from finishing it."

A brand-new motive!

Somewhere in the weeks leading up to the Expo I heard or read that most comic book artists do their drawing on computers these days, but Williams didn't. Mac was gazing at a large drafting board with a page in progress. The storyline had Kimberly Shaw, crime lab scientist by day and Red Falcon by night, encounter Professor Beatrice Beezley at a social event and begin to suspect that she is Queen Bee. In civilian clothes the supervillain didn't especially look like Winsome, the film incarnation of the character.

"Bea Beezley—what a corny name!" I couldn't help saying. I hadn't run into it before.

"That is an unfortunate predilection of the genre," Mac opined. "Batman's foe the Riddler had the given name of Edward Nygma—as in 'E. Nygma' or 'enigma'—for example."

"No excuse."

"This doesn't help us any, genius," Oscar said.

"Of course not," Mac said. "Help will be hard to find, I fear. Anything incriminating to the killer has certainly been removed from this room unless the killer was interrupted last night, of which there is no indication." Mac stroked his graying beard. "Graham Bentley Post reminded us that the works of artists become more valuable upon their demise. That will be even truer of this, Parker Williams's final work. *Cui bono?*"

In other words (English ones), who profits?

"Probably Miranda Blackwood, as the wife of the deceased," Oscar said, "except for the slight problem that her body was carried out of here this morning."

"At least we can eliminate her as a suspect," I said. "Or, rather, her killer eliminated her."

"By no means, old boy," Mac rumbled. "We could have two different murderers. We have encountered that before."

That evoked another case, and a sad memory of the one murderer I wish we hadn't caught.

"Do you think that's likely?" I asked Mac.

"Not very."

"So, who would want to kill both Parker Williams and Miranda Blackwood?"

"I heartily wish that I knew!"

Chapter Twenty-Two
Red Rage

"SPARGO TOLD US he wasn't giving up on getting that *She-Wolf* cover from the widow," I said. "Maybe he visited her last night and they had an argument that got out of hand."

"Told you when?" Oscar demanded.

"We had a brief conversation with him yesterday at Malarkey's," Mac said, which I rated as two Pinocchios at least. It wasn't that brief, and Mac managed to give the impression that we just ran into the collector rather than going to his hotel to find him.

"What else did he say that you haven't bothered to tell me?"

Mac summarized the conversation. Then he noted that by denying he killed Williams but *not* denying that he paid Red O'Connor for a forgery, Spargo was tacitly admitting to the latter. Gibbons came back into the studio just in time to get the gist of it.

"Call Spargo and tell him we want to talk to him," Oscar directed his assistant chief. Gibbons was accessing the phone number before he finished the instruction.

"Mr. Spargo? This is Erin Assistant Chief L. Jack Gibbons." I only heard one end of the interchange, but that was enough. "There has been a new development in the

Parker Williams murder case, and we would like to speak to you again. Well, I apologize for the inconvenience, but this can't wait. We'll meet you there. What time is your flight?" Mac raised an eyebrow. "That should be no problem. What airline? We'll be at the ticket counter in twenty minutes. I would advise you to be there as well."

Spargo was still squawking when Gibbons hung up.

"He was in a rental car headed to the airport," Gibbons reported.

He began moving as he spoke. We all did. Oscar and Gibbons piled into the latter's cruiser and sped, lights flashing, to the ferry with the Macmobile close behind and not observing the speed limit. We crossed over the mighty Ohio River to our neighboring state and arrived at the Cincinnati/Northern Kentucky International Airport (known as CVG) 23 minutes after we left the Williams house.

Spargo was pacing in the area where Delta passengers check in and drop off their luggage. If he'd been a cartoon, he would have had smoke pouring out of his ears. When he caught sight of our quartet approaching, he didn't wait for us to get any closer before making his opinion clear.

"This is an outrage! My plane for New York boards in an hour. Your so-called police force should be defunded." His face was almost purple. Even his Vandyke looked riled.

"Calm down," Gibbons told him. "CVG police are a little touchy about noisy guests."

"Where were you last night?" Oscar asked Spargo before the collector could respond.

"When?"

"Let's say seven to midnight."

"Living the high life at some sports bar called Bobbie McGee's."

"For five hours?"

"What else was I going to do in this one-horse town?"

There's always archery dodgeball.

"Can anybody verify that?" Gibbons asked.

He almost smiled. "A woman in a cowboy hat kept coming by to chat. She obviously had her eye on me."

"That was the owner, Bobbie McGee," I informed him. "If her eye was on you, it's because she thought you looked shifty. But you're lucky. She'll remember you, the tab, and how big a tip you left."

"Twenty percent." Spargo pulled a pocket watch out of his vest and made a show of looking at it before asking, "Now, what the living *hell* is this all about? You said something about a new development."

"Miranda Blackwood was murdered last night at Parker Williams's home," Oscar said.

Spargo said something stronger than "horse hockey," then added: "I don't know why that brings you back to me. I had no reason to kill her *or* Parker Williams. Parker exposing the forgery on exhibit in Brattleboro would have had more impact in the comic community than me doing it. And buying the original from his widow was my backup plan. I'm screwed by both deaths."

"But Ms. Blackwood declined to sell," Mac said.

"Right. I didn't give up, but I made a tactical retreat. I didn't contact her again. No, wait! I think I did call her from that sports bar after I'd had a few drinks. But I got no answer, just a recorded message that said, 'I'm not available, call back' and didn't even give her name. Here, I'll show you."

He pulled out the latest generation iPhone, selected a call with Miranda Blackwood's name on it, and noted that it only lasted 30 seconds. "Just long enough for me to say my name, tell her I'm still interested in buying—especially the *She-Wolf* cover—and asking her to call me back."

"You could have made that call to her right in front of the body," Gibbons said. "But your phone keeps a detailed map of where you've been, with a time stamp. Mind if I access it?"

"Knock yourself out. Just make it fast." He handed Gibbons the phone. "I wonder who the heirs are, and if they'd sell me the *She-Wolf?*"

"That would give you a motive to kill Ms. Blackwood, would it not?" Mac asked.

"I'm not that devious." *Color me skeptical on that point.* "Besides, that's a pretty unbelievable murder motive, even for fiction."

He looked at Mac as if he had just scored a point. But judging by the look on my brother-in-law's face, I wasn't so sure about that. I suspected that a new Damon Devlin mystery was already half-plotted in that moment.

Gibbons looked up from Spargo's phone to announce, "He didn't leave Bobbie's during the relevant time. Or at least, his phone didn't."

"Have you ever been to the Williams home?" Oscar asked.

He shook his head while he said "No."

"Print him," Oscar directed Gibbons.

That went over big.

"I haven't got time—"

"It will take you less time to comply than to continue resisting," Mac told Spargo. "Surely time is your only objection?"

The collector gave in, but not quietly. "You ought to be looking at Post," he said as Gibbons fiddled with the portable fingerprint kit. "If—when—Williams went public with his ownership of the real *She-Wolf* cover art, that was going to ruin the reputation of his little museum."

"And make it possible for you to pick up gems for your collection that otherwise might go to Brattleboro," I said.

"Your premise has a fatal flaw," Mac told Spargo. "If Graham Bentley Post slew Mr. Williams in order to cover up the fact that he had been duped by a forgery, he would scarcely have left the genuine artwork behind. Therefore—" He stopped dead, and I could see the convoluted McCabe mind at work. "Unless, of course, he brought the forgery with him and substituted it for the genuine artwork, which he then took back to Vermont. In that case, the disarray in the victim's studio would be a smokescreen to give the impression that the killer was looking for something."

"Check it out," Spargo said. "Have an expert examine what's in Parker's studio. Can I go now?"

"Go," Oscar said. "You don't want to miss your plane."

He went.

"Do you believe what you said about Post?" Gibbons asked Mac.

"Not at all. I was stating a theoretical possibility that must be considered an extreme improbability. Think of it! It beggars belief that Mr. Post would bring the forged art here from Vermont with the intention of making the substitution, then killing Parker Williams at the Expo, then somehow getting into his home later to effect the switch. Preposterous!

"Parker Williams's heir or heirs and the Library & Museum of Popular Culture own identical artworks, one of which must be counterfeit. I would suggest, however, that it would be a waste of time to 'check it out,' as Mr. Spargo urged. If the version in the Williams studio is spurious, that tells us nothing because it may have been spurious all along."

Mac looked self-satisfied at this logic, Oscar cussed, I was getting a headache, and Lt. Col. L. Jack Gibbons looked imperturbable as ever.

"What do you think?" I asked the assistant chief.

"Tough case."

"Give me a little more."

"Banfield says love, I say money." *This is what they talk about on dates?* "Her idea is that a scorned lover killed both the object of his or her affections and the person standing in the way. My idea is that when two married people die, one after the other, the second to go inherits and then somebody else inherits the whole pile."

"The ultimate heir in this case would presumably be Ms. Blackwood's son," Mac said. "He is seven years old."

Chapter Twenty-Three
RED Harvest

ON THE WAY back from the airport, before he even had time to fire up a cigar, Mac's mobile rang. He pulled the phone out of his coat pocket and handed it to me. "It's Felicity Snow," I told him as I put the speaker on and pointed the phone at Mac.

"Sebastian McCabe here!" he bellowed.

"Hey, McCabe, this is Snow. I'm totally shocked about what happened to Miranda Blackwood. I already called Chief Hummel to let him know that Gavin Frost-Pierson was home with his wife in Akron all evening and into the morning. She'll swear to that, and so will their two kids. More importantly, I know you didn't find anything to implicate my client at the house on Rachel's Way, but did you find the proof that he created the prototype of Queen Bee?"

No, but we weren't looking.

"Why do you ask me?"

"Well, it's not like Oscar the Grouch would tell me anything."

"I am not sure that I should either."

"What could it hurt?"

"I am not eager to find out."

They bandied about like that until Snow gave up, emitting a world-class sigh. "I guess it's not likely that Parker would have saved Gavin's sketch and storyline anyway. But maybe he would have. Who knows what a man who draws and writes on the edges of books might do?"

"Indeed! The thought of such a desecration horrifies me."

"Anyway, I hope you gave the place a good look. And if you didn't, you should go back and do it."

Mac disconnected shortly thereafter and ignited a rolled bundle of dried and fermented tobacco leaves to stimulate his thought process (and my coughing). I let him cogitate for a while, then I said: "What are you thinking? I know you're thinking something."

"I am thinking, Jefferson, that there is a possibility, however slim, that the killer may not have found whatever he or she was looking for, and that it might be of a nature that could have eluded Erin's finest. Please call Oscar."

What followed wasn't pretty, but the long and the short of it was that Oscar agreed to tell Officer Bertsch to let us back into the murder house and look around under her supervision. She was waiting for us outside.

"The Chief isn't happy," she said—*no spit, Sherlock!*—"but I think what you're up to is pretty cool, like a treasure hunt." In her early twenties, she'd been just a year or two ahead of Rebecca at Bernardin High. "But what exactly is it you're looking for? The Chief wasn't clear about that."

"Neither are we," I said. "A signed confession from the murderer would be nice."

Bertsch smiled, looking even younger. "I'll get right on that."

"There is one thing more to be said," Mac said. "Do you know anything about Mr. Williams's oeuvre, specifically the supervillainous character of Queen Bee? No? That is a pity. Suffice it to say that she is a master criminal who has several aspects of the queen bee, including her propensity for murdering rivals. One of our suspects in the case has alleged that he was the real creator of the character, which he called The Stinger. He says he sent a drawing to Parker Williams. If we find that, it may mean something to our case."

"Got it," Bertsch said.

"By all appearances, the killer has rifled the file cabinet, so I think we need not concern ourselves with that. Jefferson, please search the desk drawers and behind the artwork. Officer Bertsch, please check the statues for anything that might be secreted within or under, and then look through those sketchbooks. I will begin the search through these dozens of books, and then you can join me in that task when you have finished—assuming that your own explorations have been fruitless."

"Copy that," I said.

"You've been around Banfield too long," Bertsch quipped.

I started with the artwork, all of it either covers or inside pages of comic books, including that much-discussed *She-Wolf* cover. I took each one off the wall and looked at the back. None of them hid a safe. I didn't pry open any backs, not being sure that was kosher. Results: nothing, naught, nada, and also zero, zilch, zip, and zippo.

The desk was on the wall opposite the drafting board (on which still lay Williams's unfinished final Red Falcon story) so that the artist could roll back and forth between the two in his chair. Appropriately enough, the desktop was occupied in part by a desktop computer, the contents of which would take more than a quick rumble to reveal. Ignoring that, I moved to the four drawers. They largely contained more of what was also on the top: pens, pencils, paper clips, tape, blank notebooks, staplegun, staples, and mailing envelopes. I picked up one of the mailing envelopes to look inside when I heard:

"I found something!"

Mac, who was holding an oversized volume called *The Paragon Encyclopedia*, and I both looked up.

Bertsch held in her right hand a piece of paper that I could see had been folded in half before she opened it. "It was inside this sketchbook full of random drawings." The book was about eight inches by ten inches.

The image in the drawing, rather crudely done but much better than I could produce, was a woman with a cone-shaped hairdo and a horizontally striped one-piece costume of yellow and black. Right below her high heels were the initials *G.F-P.*

"That hair style is called a beehive," Bertsch said. "It was popular in the '60s." *As if we didn't know that.*

At the top of the drawing were the words **"The Stinger!"** On the right was a column of phrases constituting a quick verbal sketch of the character:

> **Wheelhouse:** *Criminal mastermind*
> **Day job:** *Entomology professor (Sheila Clark)*
> **Distinguishing characteristic:** *Eliminates all rivals (like a queen bee)*
> **M.O.:** *Kills with bee venom*

"Well done, Officer Bertsch!" Mac told her.

"I got lucky," she said, truthfully.

"But no second page, an outline of a story?" I asked. Bertsch shook her head. "Just this."

"Mr. Williams might have discarded that as unpromising, if all is as it appears," Mac said.

"How does it appear?" Bertsch asked. "I mean, what is this?"

"On its face, it is significant evidence—one might even say proof—that Gavin Frost-Pierson did essentially create the character now known as Queen Bee. That might mean that he killed Mr. Williams out of righteous anger, and then slew Ms. Blackwood while attempting unsuccessfully to find this after she admitted him to the home.

"Alternatively, however, it could be that Mr. Frost-Pierson drew this recently and planted it after killing Ms. Blackwood. After all, it is not carbon dated and we know from his false claims of death threats against him that he is capable of deceit. In that case, he could still be the murderer on the premise that he hoped to establish his claims and win a financial settlement from the Williams estate, which might be more amenable to that than either husband or wife."

Bertsch, being new to the perambulations of the McCabe brain, just stared. Then she asked, "Where does that leave us?"

"With a lot of theories," I told her. "This discovery will thrill Frost-Pierson and his lawyer until they realize it doesn't rule him out as a double murder suspect."

Mac closed *The Paragon Encyclopedia* and shelved it next to two similar volumes devoted to the Marvel and DC universes. "Ah, this looks promising." He picked up a copy of Dashiell Hammett's *Red Harvest*, one of the two Hammett books whose titles Williams said inspired the name Red Falcon. It was a nice edition with an imitation leather cover, but not in the league of my *Kiss Me, Deadly* first edition from Lynda. After flipping through to see if anything was tucked inside, as it had been with the sketchbook, Mac looked on the edge of the book—the side that was opposite the spine.

"By thunder, there is something!" he roared.

The "something" was writing:

I fear RED.

"Red again," I said.

"Not 'red,' old boy—R-E-D. Those three letters, unlike the word before them, are all capitalized. When are several letters together capitalized? When they're an acronym or initials."

"So, does anybody in this case have those initials?" Bertsch asked.

That's when I saw it.

"Yeah," I said, "Rita Ellison Daponte, Parker Williams's 'just a fling.'"

Chapter Twenty-Four
Red Light

"I'LL HAVE GIBBONS bring her in," Oscar told Mac over the phone.

"I am by no means convinced—" Mac began.

"Neither am I. Yet." Oscar hung up.

Now I have to relate events as reported to me by Lt. Col. L. Jack Gibbons, which means I would bet my combined IRA and 403(b) balances on the accuracy of the account.

After some discussion with Oscar at the police station in the presence of several others (that's an important detail), Gibbons decided to drop in on Rita Daponte at the Public Library of Erin and Sussex County without calling first. He arrived just in time to see her hurrying down the front steps of the brick-and-stone Andrew Carnegie building on Mulberry Street.

"Mrs. Daponte!" Gibbons called.

She looked his way, saw him, and immediately hustled into a 2014 silver Honda Civic parked in front of the library.

As classic newspaperese would put it, Gibbons "gave chase" with his blue lights and siren on, although at about only 35 miles an hour because they were in the heart of downtown. They turned right on Front Street, right on Court (past the police station), and left on Main before Rita Daponte stopped at a red light on Vine and pressed her head against the steering wheel. Gibbons parked behind her with his lights still flashing, approached her car, and knocked on the door. She sat up and rolled down the driver's side.

"We need to talk to you," Gibbons told her.

"I PANICKED," RITA explained in Oscar's conference room, flanked by her husband and her attorney, Erica Slade of the newly rebranded firm SladeLaw. Mrs. Daponte wore a knit sweater about the same shade of blue as her eyes. "It was stupid, stupid, stupid."

Nobody disagreed. Even Slade, Erin's leading defense attorney, was silent, biding her time.

"You were already fleeing when I arrived at the library," Gibbons said. "How did you know I was coming to talk with you?"

"A friend—I won't say who—told me that, and also that Miranda Blackwood was murdered, just to give me a heads-up. Running was my own stupid idea."

"Warning you was also a stupid idea and if I find out who did it, somebody will be looking for a new job." Oscar said it loud enough to carry down the hall, which was no doubt his intention.

"Running made me look guilty, didn't it?" Rita Daponte said.

Oscar tried his hand at understatement: "You could say that."

"As the old saying goes, appearances are deceiving," Slade said.

"I shouldn't have even called it an idea," her client went on. "It was more like an impulse. When it comes to fight or flight, I take flight every time."

"And why did you stop that flight?" Mac inquired.

"I always stop at red lights."

"Clearly, my client is a perfectly law-abiding citizen," Slade said. Charming at social events and over drinks at Bobbie McGee's, she is hell-on-high-heels in a courtroom. She has long dark hair, bright violet eyes, and the build of the gym teacher and Bengals cheerleader that she once was. "Ms. Daponte very much regrets her poor decision to get into her car and drive away as Colonel Gibbons approached. I certainly hope you aren't serious about a charge of unlawful flight, Chief."

"That depends on how this goes," that worthy said.

"Let me repeat what I said when I arrived: My client has nothing to hide and will fully cooperate. She has no reason not to, because she had no motivation to kill either of the victims."

"How about she was still in love with Parker Williams and she couldn't have him?" Gibbons said. "That's a motive to kill him and the woman who had him."

You may recall that was a theory Mac and I tossed around and then discarded before the Blackwood murder, leaving Rita Daponte off of our motive chart.

"Preposterous!" Slade snorted. "Soap opera stuff." That seemed a little rich to me, given that her own romantic affairs are a bit tangled and well known about town. County Prosecutor Marvin Slade's roving eye is the reason he's her ex-husband, although there are indications that the old fires between them are burning again, and I don't mean the heat of their courtroom battles.

Rita Daponte looked at her husband, who looked back in a way that made me want to say *Rent a room, you two!* "I didn't love Parker. It was just a stupid mistake I made because I was feeling neglected at home and flattered by his attention. I used to hate Parker for what I did, but I'm over that now. It was my own fault. I own it. I've been talking to Sister Polly about that." She fingered the crucifix at her neck.

Sister Mary Margaret Malone—Triple M—is not a marriage counselor, but her spiritual direction has been known to have positive marital effects. My own marriage is one of them in a roundabout way through her friendship with Lynda. And as a volunteer chaplain at the police station lockup, she could have overheard the Oscar-Gibbons dialogue and alerted Rita Ellison Daponte that Gibbons was headed her way. But I've never asked.

"Our family is still messed up, and we're working hard on un-messing it together," the suspect continued. "Jennifer—that's our daughter—is being treated for anxiety and depression, like a lot of kids her age who post sexy videos on TikTok. She needs two highly involved parents and that's us." I know less about the TikTok video hosting service than I do about cryptocurrency (almost nothing), but I'd heard that sort of thing before. On the other hand, Shalimar Burton used TikTok as one of her ways to spread positive empowerment messages. I made a mental note to get Riley St. Simon to tutor me on it.

"But none of that is any of your business," Al Daponte spoke up. He looked up and down our side of the conference table to include both professionals and amateurs sitting there.

"Did you threaten Mr. Williams?" Mac asked Rita.

"What? No way!"

"Why do you ask?" Slade demanded.

Oscar pulled his trump card. "Parker Williams wrote a message on the edge of a book called *Red Harvest*. It says, 'I fear R-E-D.'" He spelled out the letters. "Those are your initials, Mrs. Daponte."

From the wide-eyed, slack-jawed expression on her face, she was either shocked or a better actor than any of the professionals we'd encountered.

"A coincidence," Slade snapped before her client could say anything. "Why would Williams write her initials when he could have written 'Rita' with one more letter? And who calls her 'Rita Ellison Daponte' anyway? And what about the woman in red that I keep reading about?"

Oscar could say, "I'm the one asking the questions here," but that would be a cliché.

"I'm the one asking the questions here," Oscar said.

"And my client has answered them." Slade made a show of sounding exasperated. "Do you have any more?"

"Where were you at the time of the Blackwood murder?" Gibbons asked Rita Daponte.

"What time was that?" Slade riposted.

This is like ping-pong with words.

"The time doesn't matter if it was after six o'clock," Rita Daponte said, ignoring her counsel. "That's when Al got home. I made dinner for us and Jennifer, then Al and I watched TV until we went to bed at eleven. We don't normally watch that much but we're still reeling from the weekend, and we felt like zoning out."

"That's all true," Daponte said.

"What did you watch?"

"We binged on the latest season of *Vera*," his wife said. "The first three out of six episodes."

"That doesn't help much," Oscar said. "I happen to know that those shows were streamed a while back. A friend of mine"—that would be Popcorn—"watched all of them last month. You could have done the same."

"But we didn't," Daponte said. "I'll take a lie detector test."

"Clearly no husband would lie to protect a woman who killed a former lover for the fantasy motive that you suggest," Slade told our side of the table. "However, I would never let a client take a polygraph test. They are notoriously unreliable."

"I'm not your client," Daponte said. "Rita is."

"You hired me."

"Which raises an interesting question," Oscar said. "Why did you lawyer up your wife so fast, Daponte?"

"I figured you'd get the bright idea of hauling her in after these two"—he indicated Mac and me—"had a little chat with me on Monday night."

"Oh, they did, did they?" Oscar turned his head and gave us a look that would have frozen a geyser. No doubt he thought we should have filled him in.

"Can I get back to my job now?" Rita asked. "I don't want to get fired. We need the health insurance."

Slade stood up. "I think we're done here."

The Dapontes also stood up, but Gibbons had a final question: "Your alibi for the Williams murder is that you were working for your husband at his store on Saturday. Do you recall any customers at that time who can vouch for seeing you, or made a credit card purchase so the time can be traced?"

"From what I read in the *Observer*, that must have been around four o'clock or so, right?" Rita shook her head of light brown hair. "The place was dead." *Bad choice of words.* "I told Al it would be. The store is ten minutes away from a Comic Book Expo, which is to comic geeks what honey is to flies. Who would play bingo at a church hall when you can go to the Forty Thieves casino?"

"SHE HAS WEAK alibis for both murders," Gibbons commented after they'd left.

"And she was practically named by the victim— twice," Oscar piled on.

"You accept the message written on the copy of *Red Harvest*, seemingly her initials, as genuine, then?" Mac said.

"Hell's bells, why shouldn't I? It's just the kind of nutty thing a guy who reads mysteries and made a living drawing chesty women in tight suits might do." *I'm not sure I get the connection there.* "Besides, doesn't it make sense that if he already wrote that on the book earlier it would be on his mind to write something similar to identify his killer after he'd been stabbed? He already had RED in his mental attic."

"A nice image, Oscar, I must say!"

"You're the one who found the message on the book, Mac. Why aren't you taking a victory lap?"

"Because it offends my olfactory sense." *Meaning it doesn't smell right.* "If Mr. Williams really were afraid, he would have told someone, not written a hidden message unlikely to ever be found."

"Maybe he told Miranda," I threw back. "I'm with Oscar. I don't get your attitude. Another case with a dying message from a murder victim should suit you down to the ground, as the Brits say."

"That is exactly what unsettles me, old boy. It fits me all too well, as if it were by design. I also refuse to believe that a killer fleeing the police would stop for a red light as Mrs. Daponte did."

Oscar shook his head in disagreement. "People do the damnedest things."

I couldn't argue with that.

"At any rate," Mac said, "I suggest that we keep this latest bit of RED to ourselves for now. Only we, the killer, and the Dapontes know about it. That might be helpful."

"The killer and Rita Daponte are the same person," Oscar said, "but I'll play along. What Rawls doesn't know won't hurt her. This isn't like the Williams murder, where we wanted the help of the public in figuring out the meaning of the message."

Mac's phone rang. Seeing who it was, he answered. "Sebastian McCabe here!"

"Did you find anything at Parker's house?" Felicity Snow wanted to know, not speaking softly.

With the RED message off the table, Mac told the truth but not the whole truth, which he insists is not the same as lying: "Of interest to your client, we did indeed discover what appears to be an early sketch of the character now known as Queen Bee."

"What? That's fantastic!" Snow did all but whoop.

"Why do you sound so surprised, Ms. Snow? You are the one who urged us to look for it."

"Yeah, but I was just pissing in the wind. I knew Gavin sent his drawing and notes about The Stinger to

Parker, but I didn't really think Parker would be so stupid as to hold on to it. I hoped for it, but I didn't really expect it."

"Nor should you have," Mac said. "Why would a plagiarist keep the evidence of his infraction?"

"The Parker I knew was capable of forgetting things—the fact that he was married, for one—so maybe he just put it somewhere out of sight and out of mind. And later on, he convinced himself that the supervillain with the piled-up hair was his own idea. Where did you find the drawing?"

"In a sketchbook."

"That explains it, then. Parker had dozens of those lying around, and probably hadn't opened that one for years."

"You will forgive me for suggesting that the surfacing of this artifact after the Williams murder is a bit too convenient. Your client can pursue his claims of plagiarism against the estate, which will be at a disadvantage without Mr. Williams being alive to defend himself. And, in fact, it is far from impossible that this apparent evidence of plagiarism is nothing of the sort but, rather, of quite recent origin."

"What are you implying?"

"Merely that Gavin Frost-Pierson could have slain Parker Williams, either out of animus or avarice, then been forced to resort to homicide again when he was interrupted by Ms. Blackwood in the course of planting that drawing of 'The Stinger,' which could have been made at any time."

Oscar rolled his eyes but kept silent.

Snow gave a hollow laugh. "You read too many detective stories. And you also don't know my client very well. Are we off the record here?"

"Certainly." *Never mind that the Chief of Police is listening.* "Unless, of course, you intend to confess to double murder."

"Not today. Okay, then, there are three problems with your scenario. Number one, Gavin isn't devious enough to think of hiding false evidence in Parker's house, or capable of actually doing it."

I grabbed the phone. "Not devious? Frost-Pierson invented death threats against himself to gain attention to his plagiarism claim."

"A claim now verified. That death-threat business was a stupid maneuver which came back to bite him in the ass. Which brings me to my point number two: I've gotten to know Gavin as a sweet but hapless man. He could screw up a one-car parade. And that's what he did when he sent an inspired creative idea to Parker without protecting himself. By the way, you said you found something of interest to my client. Did you come up with anything else in that house?"

"Why do you ask?"

"Why don't you answer?"

"You should be a lawyer, Ms. Snow." *I wish I'd said that.*

"Very funny, McCabe. All right, then, don't tell me what you found. I'll use my imagination."

"What is the third point in exculpation of your client?"

"What you already know: That Gavin was with his family in Akron at the time of the murder. Check out Kit Frost-Pierson's Facebook page for some wonderful pictures of them celebrating son Jeffrey's ninth birthday."

After Snow disconnected, Oscar said, "Convinced?"

"She makes a powerful series of arguments," Mac conceded.

"And she didn't even mention point four," I said.

Oscar's face was a question mark.

"No forced entry," Mac told him. "If Gavin Frost-Pierson was interrupted by Miranda Blackwood while planting that drawing, how did he get into the house?"

"Just for the sake of argument, I said before the killer could have found a key hidden under a mat or some other stupid hiding place."

Mac raised an eyebrow. "So you did. And right you are. Thank you, Oscar!"

NEWS TRAVELS FAST in Erin. When I got home that night, Rita Daponte's friend (and ours) Sister Mary Margaret Malone greeted me in the hallway. Triple M stops by often to visit Lynda and the kids, but this time she wanted to see me. Her normally cheerful visage was marked by worry-lines that uncharacteristically made her look every bit of her 43 years and then some. Even her bangs looked wilted.

"You and Mac have to save her," she said.

"Rita Daponte, you mean?"

"Who else? She didn't kill anybody. I'm sure of it. I know her soul. Rita's a good person who knows she did a bad thing and is trying to make up for it."

I'd seldom seen Triple M so agitated.

"Drink this," Lynda ordered, handing her a glass of Roadhouse Red.

"Just to be the devil's advocate," I said—maybe a poor choice of words—"Oscar might say that's her motive for killing Williams, that she blamed him for seducing her." *Never mind the "if I can't have him no one can" jealous woman theory, which also accounts for the Blackwood murder.*

Triple M took a gulp of the red wine. "Rita doesn't blame anyone but herself for what happened. She had zero reason to murder anybody. Trust me on that."

Chapter Twenty-Five
Red Corvette

THE MORNING CHAOS at the Cody house had barely begun the next day, Thursday, when the doorbell rang at 6:48 A.M. I was the closest to the door, so I opened it. Johanna Rawls handed me that day's edition of the *Erin Observer & News-Ledger.*

"You were having a delivery issue, so I wanted to be sure you got the paper."

"That's what I call service, but it wasn't really—"

"Johanna!" That was Lynda, three kids in tow. Tall Rawls immediately descended to the little ones' level and started hugging and talking to them. It occurred to me, not for the first time, that she has strong maternal instincts not yet deployed to fullest effect. On the other hand, she's a year younger than Lynda was when Donata was born, so she still has some time on her biological clock. None of my business anyway! Making a mental note to not think about that, I opened the *Observer* to read the story headlined **STAR MUR-DERED, SUSPECT FLEES.**

By Johanna Rawls
Hollywood star Miranda Blackwood was found dead Wednesday morning in the Erin

home of her late husband, comic book writer-artist Parker Williams, who was murdered on Saturday at the Tri-State Comic Expo.

Erin resident Rita Ellison Daponte, wanted for questioning in connection with the murders, led Assistant Police Chief L. Jack Gibbons on a brief low-speed chase through downtown Erin before giving herself up. She was taken in for questioning and then released. Police Chief Oscar Hummel called her a "person of interest" but declined to say why.

"My client is fully cooperating with the police because she has nothing to hide," said Ms. Daponte's attorney, Erica Slade.

Asked about the relationship between Ms. Daponte and the dead couple, both Hummel and Slade declined to comment.

The story went on for eighteen more paragraphs with details about Kyle Rufus finding the body, but not a word about "I fear RED." Oscar had bowed to Mac's wish to keep that under wraps.

"'Low-speed chase,'" I commented. "Cute."

"Thanks," Johanna said, standing up to almost my height. "What can you tell me about a message left by Parker Williams that the Chief thinks points to Rita Daponte?"

Uh-oh!

"What can you tell me about when you're going to marry Seth?" I countered.

Lynda glowered, but Tall Rawls ignored my riposte. "Come on, Jeff, throw me a bone here."

"Because Oscar won't?"

"You could say that. He wouldn't confirm that the phrase 'I fear R-E-D,' those being Ms. Daponte's initials, was found written on the edges of a book in the victim's house. So, I left it out of the story until I can get a second source, such as you or Mac."

"Where did you hear about this alleged writing on an alleged book?"

"That's confidential."

"How about just the first name?"

The reporter sighed. "The truth is, I wish I knew. I received an anonymous tip emailed from a Yahoo address including the word 'tipster.' So, if I run with this 'I fear RED' thing, will I regret it in the morning?"

I gave my impression of a Mona Lisa smile.

"Nice try, Johanna," Lynda said. "Hey, you don't look like your normal cheerful self. What's wrong?"

"Working this story is the hardest thing I ever had to do in journalism," she said. "Rita is an old friend of mine, going back to high school. I was her big sister—a senior when she was a freshman. But I couldn't let that influence my reporting on her arrest."

"What was she like in high school?" I wondered.

"The same as now—insecure. Do you really think she did it?"

"Mac doesn't."

"MAC STOPPED BY," Popcorn informed me when I walked in the door a short time later at our Gamble Building digs.

"In person? He must have needed the exercise."

We both laughed.

"He said for you to go see him as soon as you get in."

"What, am I supposed to be at his beck and call?"

Not answering that, she got very busy at her computer. While I was standing there trying to decide whether to ignore Mac's summons, my mobile rang. I was surprised to see that the caller was Mary Lou Springfield.

"I told you it was that Rita Daponte," she said without preamble.

"You said it was Al Daponte."

"Whatever. The point is, the murder was all about the Williams-Daponte affair."

"Mac isn't convinced that Rita's guilty."

"I knew he'd be stubborn about this. That's why I called you instead of him."

Before I could craft a response that was both truthful and loyal to Mac, Roscoe Feldman came on the line.

"I still say it was Jessica Ballantine," he said.

"She has an alibi for the Williams murder and no conceivable reason for killing Miranda Blackwood," I informed him.

"Well, I guess you have me there."

Springfield took over her phone again. "Mac's had a good run, but nobody's right all the time."

I couldn't argue with that, so I just said, "Have a good day, Mary Lou."

In no mood to see Mac after that, I trudged into my office. It occurred to me that if we could get Saylor-Mackie to work a budgetary miracle that would allow the hiring of Riley St. Simon and maybe even Sylvester Link, we would have to reconfigure our rabbit warren. Maybe we could get the institutional advancement troops moved to another floor.

Popcorn and I talked about that a bit over coffee, then I spent an hour working on a GK speech to the National Association of Independent Colleges and Universities. After that, figuring that I'd dragged my feet enough to assert my independence, I hoofed it over to Herbert Hall.

"Ah, Jefferson, had a busy morning, have you?" Mac boomed from behind the computer at his desk.

I cut to the chase, bringing him news instead of responding to the implied criticism: "Looks like Oscar has a mole in his troops. Unless you sent Johanna an anonymous tip telling her about the *Red Harvest* clue. Somebody did. And by the way, Triple M is in your corner, thoroughly disbelieving that Rita Daponte bashed Williams."

When I had unloaded all that, Mac stroked his facial follicles. "The player on the other side has overplayed his or her hand, old boy."

"Eh? What does that mean in English?"

"It means that not only do I believe Mrs. Daponte is innocent, I also still do *not* believe the 'RED' message on that book was left by Parker Williams. If he had chosen that singularly obscure method of expressing fear for his life, why would he write Mrs. Daponte's initials rather than simply name her? Similarly, as Erica Slade said, if she were the killer why would Mr. Williams not write the name "Rita" in that notebook as he was facing death instead of "RED"? Surely not to keep her from recognizing the message as pointing to her. Rita Ellison Daponte, in her guilt—were she guilty—undoubtedly would see her own initials in RED as easily as she would see her name."

"Well, maybe she just happened to be disguised in something red and . . ." I petered out as Mac shook his head.

"I accept that Parker Williams tried to indicate his killer by scrawling a simple description on that sketchpad in his dying moments. I am equally certain, however, that he was not the author of what we are supposed to believe was another message from him written at his leisure and left at his home in an obscure location in case he should perish at the hand of a woman he feared. He did that instead of calling the police or telling his wife, who certainly would have informed us if he had done so? Bosh!"

"Watch your language. Maybe he didn't have enough evidence to go to the police and he was afraid to get laughed at."

"And, therefore, he wrote his concern on the edges of a book? That strains credulity."

Says the creator of Damon Devlin, magician-sleuth solver of impossible crimes.

"So," I said, "just to clarify, the second clue doesn't mean anything, except that maybe the killer is trying to throw us off the track from the meaning of the first clue, or maybe giving us a scapegoat for the murder by using Rita Daponte's initials." *I think I got that right.*

Mac nodded. "More likely the latter than the former."

"Good point, since we're not really on a track to be thrown off of."

"Or perhaps we have already thrown ourselves off. I have a nagging feeling that I was on to something early in this case that I failed to follow through when we drowned in a red sea of possible meanings for Parker Williams's dying message. My instinct tells me that the solution to his murder, and therefore his wife's, is simpler than it seems."

I was about to second that notion, given that it could hardly be more complicated, when Oscar called to crow. Mac didn't need to turn on the speaker for me to hear the triumph in the Chief's voice. He just held the phone out.

"The BCI[15] reports that Spargo's fingerprints don't match any that we picked up in the Williams house, but Rita Daponte's do," he said. "She was at the crime scene."

I expected Mac to lift an eyebrow at that, but he was unmoved.

"Surely that is hardly significant," he said. "There is no way to tell how long ago Mrs. Daponte left those prints.[16] She had a liaison with the victim that could well have involved visits to his home in the absence of his then-wife, Ms. Manders. Undoubtedly, the prints of all three of Mr. Williams's wives are in that house, and perhaps those of other women as well. I regret to report that some married men who stray apparently enjoy the added thrill associated with doing so in their own home. Or so I hear. Incidentally, Jefferson and I visited that home during the Fourth of July murder case in 2017. If you find our fingerprints there, please do not incarcerate us."

I thought that was laying it on a little thick, but Oscar took it in stride.

"Oh, I don't know, Mac, since you two are the least likely suspects, you probably would be the killers if this was one of your mysteries."

---

[15] The Ohio Bureau of Criminal Investigation, the state's crime lab, serves law enforcement throughout the state.

[16] At this writing, the Missouri State Highway Patrol notes on its website that "fingerprints have been developed on surfaces that had not been touched in over forty years; yet not developed on a surface that was handled very recently."—*S. McC.*

Touché!

Mac ignored that, rolling on with his argument that if Williams feared for his life, he would have done something about it other than write initials on the edge of a book. "I am not even sure why I searched in a place so unlikely."

"Meanwhile, back on Planet Earth," Oscar said, "I'm going to bring back Mrs. Daponte for another guest appearance."

"Along with Erica Slade, no doubt," I reminded him.

"But not with you two skeptics. Gibbons and I can handle this return match on our own, thanks."

"And what do you posit as Mrs. Daponte's motive for killing Ms. Blackwood?"

"Obviously, she was caught in the house looking for anything that might incriminate her in Williams's murder. Just her tough luck she didn't find it."

After a little more of this and that, Mac disconnected. "We had best accelerate our efforts lest friend Oscar make a bad mistake." At this point Mac had everything he needed to solve both murders, but of course he didn't know that. He drummed his pudgy fingers on the paper-piled desk until he came up with: "Before Oscar called, we were speaking as if the situation were either/or. It is not."

"Meaning?"

"If Parker Williams wrote that message in *Red Harvest*, it only makes sense that he would have also told someone about his fear. Therefore, if he did *not* do so, that is negative evidence against the authenticity of the supposed indictment of Mrs. Daponte. If he genuinely feared for his life, to whom might he express that other than to his wife and the police?"

I gave that a think. "Maybe his agent or his editor—they wouldn't want to see him dead."

"And locally?"

"He had no children and I gather that he didn't mingle much in Erin, except maybe at Vinyl."

Mac thumped his desk. "By thunder, yes!"

THE LITTLE STORE called Vinyl, at the corner of Market and Broadway, is where Mac and I first encountered Williams looking through LPs on a July day almost five years earlier. The store inventory is mostly used records, but also includes some surprisingly recent releases for die-hard vinyl fans.

"Yeah," store owner George Peebles agreed with Mac's premise. "I guess you could say Parker and I were friends. He sure spent a lot of time here, at least once or twice a week, and we yakked while he looked through whatever was new since his last visit. And he didn't just window-shop. His demise is going to be a hit to my bottom line."

I wasn't sure that the wire-rimmed Peebles had cut his long gray hair since our last visit, but he'd swapped out his Rolling Stones T-shirt for an Abbey Road sweatshirt.

"Without going into details," Mac said, "there is some indication that Mr. Williams might have been in fear for his life. Did he ever express that to you in words during your conversations, or in any other way give you reason to believe that was the case?"

"What? You mean like he knew he was going to be murdered? No. That's crazy, man."

"Did he seem worried about anything?"

Peebles hesitated. "Well, 'worried' might not be the word for it. But he was pissed, for sure. I made the mistake of asking him a couple of weeks ago about something I heard from another regular, that some other writer claimed Parker stole one of his characters. He didn't take that too well."

"What did he say?"

"Something about the guy who accused him was a loser and—I remember this part—'losers always lose.' And then something about how he'd like to get him in a dark alley. I can see what you're thinking and you're right: Parker was one of my best customers, but not the nicest."

"Individuals who get themselves murdered often are not," Mac observed.

So, no indication that Williams was afraid somebody was measuring him for a casket. I tried to wring something else out of this conversation.

"I'm sure you've read that Parker scrawled the words 'woman' and 'red' as he was dying," I told Peebles. "We're assuming that's what he saw before he died. Can you imagine any other significance of those words to Parker Williams?"

"Well," said Peebles with a half-smile, "he did like women. Probably too much. As for red, how about the group Red Hot Chili Peppers? He liked them. Or maybe the song 'Little Red Corvette' by Prince—I sold him that LP."

That's about as relevant as Sebastian McCabe's red 1959 Chevy Convertible with the fuzzy dice hanging off the mirror.

"Not exactly what I had in mind," I told him.

"You did say to imagine," Mac chastised me. "Mr. Peebles, who do you think might have wanted to kill Parker Williams?"

He shrugged. "A jealous husband, maybe? Like I said, he liked women."

Chapter Twenty-Six
Red Flag

"JEALOUS HUSBAND at least gets us further than 'Little Red Corvette,'" I commented to Mac that evening in the McCabe man cave. "Maybe we should take a closer look at Al Daponte."

"You posit that he sought retribution against Parker Williams for his wife's brief affair years ago, as Mary Lou Springfield suggested?"

Instead of updating Mac on the Springfield-Feldman phone call, during which Mary Lou claimed Rita's presumed guilt as a vindication, I responded with:

"'Revenge is a dish best served cold,' as the old Klingon proverb says. But if you don't like Daponte for the murder, how about the unknown father of Miranda Blackwood's son? He might have the revenge motive *and* indirectly benefit financially from the murders when his son presumably inherits."

I was on fire, but Mac doused the flames by saying, "What, then, is the meaning of 'red'?"

"Well, um, hmmm." Or words to that effect. I had nothing.

"In the PublicEye online community of would-be sleuths, the person known as Bethany Lane—which I suspect is a nom de plume for someone in Erin—has broken the news about the writing on *Red Harvest*."

"If she—assuming Bethany is a 'she'—knows about that 'I fear RED' business, Oscar might as well call a news conference. I wonder how she found out—the same inside source who tipped Johanna, maybe?"

"Moreover," Mac steamed on, "the pseudonymous Ms. Lane is vigorously promoting the scenario that RED stands for Rita Ellison Daponte's initials. That alone is a red flag that the truth lies elsewhere, given the PublicEye community's poor track record at crime solving."

"Bunch of amateurs," I quipped. "On the other hand, maybe they are overdue to stumble onto the truth."

Mac quaffed a beer and fiddled with his beard. "You will recall that in her earlier musings, Bethany Lane pushed rather hard for the theory that the killer was dressed as Red Falcon. She urged authorities to seek out such by looking at photos and videos of the Expo."

"Which Oscar's troops did, but without finding anyone who had a logical, or even illogical, reason for disposing of the Falcon's creator."

He nodded. "She also urged looking for red jewelry, hats, shoes, dresses, pantsuits, scarves, and tattoos."

"In other words, anything that could possibly be red."

"Not quite, old boy. Reviewing that list this afternoon was helpful to me because I realized what it omitted—a noun to which the adjective 'red' can be and fairly often is applied, a word that occurred to me almost immediately on Saturday. Unfortunately, it quickly slipped off my radar as we pursued what seemed to be more likely scenarios. You will recall I said yesterday that I had what I called a nagging feeling I was on to something earlier in this case. Now I know what it was."

You probably see it, but I didn't until Mac laid it out for me.

"Red hair," he said.

"I'll be damned!" I said.

"I sincerely hope not!"

"You're saying Williams's killer was one of my fellow redheads."

"Almost certainly not."

I hate it when he does that.

"Given that it is unlikely that one would be carrying a lethal weapon by happenstance, the murder of Parker Williams smacks of premeditation," Mac reminded me. "If you were intent on murder, in a venue in which many of the other participants were in costume, would you fail to disguise yourself? I thought not. The red hair was most likely a wig, which was quickly discarded. Oscar has agreed, after pro forma grumbling, to have his officers search for a discarded hairpiece in the Towne Center and nearby. My hope is that if one is found, it may yield a clue as to who donned it."

My head was spinning like a politician's press officer. "If the killer wore a wig, then we can't know who she was. So, why would the killer try to undercut Williams's genuine 'red' message by leaving a false one on that book at the scene of Miranda Blackwood's murder, according to your theory? Anybody could be hiding under a red wig."

"Ah, there's the rub, Jefferson! I have not yet thought that out."

"Well, that's a refreshing admission, but it's not going to help us much with either murder." Clearly, I was going to have to step up here. I put the Cody mind in gear as I nursed a Caffeine-Free Diet Coke. And I found myself focusing on the second murder.

"Oscar thinks Blackwood interrupted Rita Daponte in the process of trying to find incriminating evidence, i.e., the message on the book," I said. "Obviously, that doesn't work for us. So, why was Blackwood killed?

"Let's go back to the chart of motives you created for the Williams murder. It included self-preservation, payback, financial gain, and love. We'll start with self-preservation and work our way left. If Blackwood was a threat to somebody, there's no way of knowing whom. That's possible, but no help to us. Payback? We know Blackwood wasn't great pals with her co-star, but it's hard to believe Winsome would track Blackwood down at the Williams house because of some Hollywood feud—or that anybody else with an axe to grind would, for that matter. And besides, those motives only work for Blackwood, not for killing her *and* Williams. Financial gain? We don't know who gets her money and what she inherited from Williams other than, presumably, her young son. Skip that for now. Love? That's more promising. You know, we never really ruled out the possibility that Sarah-Jane Manders killed her ex-husband and his current wife out of the old woman-scorned motive. What do you think?"

"I think we have a great deal more thinking to do."

And he did it.

"WHY DOESN'T OSCAR arrest Rita Daponte if he's so sure she's the killer?" Kate asked Mac.

"Marvin Slade warned him to hold off until he has stronger evidence," I horned in. "Oscar thinks Slade doesn't want to face his ex in court with an empty hand, presuming that Erica is counsel for the defense." I knew this because Oscar told Popcorn and Popcorn told me on Friday morning. The current conversation was on Sunday during after-Mass brunch at the McCabes' house, served up by Chef Sebastian.

Frank Woodford's recently-launched "To Be Frank" column in that morning's *Observer* hit hard at the "Why haven't our public servants"—meaning Oscar—"caught the double killer?" theme. That's what launched this gabfest. Frank, the former managing director of the paper, is having a ball in his new role as "editor at large," which means he gets to pontificate in print and no longer has to run anything.

"The prosecutor is doing Oscar a favor," Mac opined as he unloaded omelets onto our plates. "Mrs. Daponte is not the killer."

"How do you know that?" Lynda asked.

"Because someone wants us to think she is." Mac dished out his own breakfast and sat down. After leading the table in the meal prayer, he said, "I have a fresh notion of my own—highly speculative, but intriguing."

"If you do say so yourself," Kate said.

Mac ignored her.

"Suppose that Miranda Blackwood was the primary victim. Suppose that her husband was only killed by a woman in red, if it was a woman, (a) to camouflage the fact that Ms. Blackwood was the real target, or (b) to make it easier for her to be the target—by luring her to the Williams home, for example—or, (c) best reason of all, so that Ms. Blackwood would inherit from Parker Williams and therefore her subsequent death would in turn benefit an heir. Whoever that heir might be in addition to her son."

"That's a lot of supposing," I objected. "And where does the writing on the side of that book at Williams's house fit in?"

Mac caffeinated himself, then said, "What was the result of that message, Jefferson? It pointed us toward Mrs. Daponte, who has become Oscar's primary suspect. Perhaps that was the intention all along."

"Well, that probably leaves out the father of Miranda Blackwood's child, whoever he is," Lynda said. "I mean, he's presumably some Hollywood type who wouldn't even know Rita Daponte, much less that her initials are R.E.D."

"Still," Kate said, "who might have been the father of her child and also at the Expo?"

"Llewellyn Chase was the only male actor at the Expo that I'd ever heard of," I said.

"His name was bandied about a bit on PublicEye last week, though not by the person known as Bethany Lane," Mac said. "Perhaps I should have paid closer attention, although I do not recall any paternity speculation."

"As the organizer of the Expo, Al Daponte could tell you how to reach Chase," I said. "I'm sure he'd be happy to help."

Chapter Twenty-Seven
Red-Hot Gossip

THERE'S NO REAL off day in my line of work, given
that I'm paid in part to field media calls 24/7. Still, I was looking forward to a quiet President's Day when I sat down to a
late breakfast the next morning. I expected to catch up on a
little office work, having slacked off a bit on that during the
previous week, then maybe watch a movie with Lynda and
the kids. A nap might have fit in there somewhere as well. I
was glancing at the headline of Tall Rawls's page 3A feature
story in the *Observer* on the Williams-Blackwood marriage
(**ERIN MEETS HOLLYWOOD**), when my phone rang.

"Please don't tell me there's a safety emergency on
campus," I said by way of greeting.

"Hi, Jeff," Banfield said. "Don't worry, I'm not even
working today. I just became privy to a little info that I
thought you'd like to hear. A certain friend of the male per-
suasion"—that would be Gibbons—"tells me that Miranda
Blackwood's lawyer, a guy named Harry Schwartz, will be in
town today to work on some estate stuff and he's going to
meet with Chief Hummel. I thought you and Seb would be
interested."

"We are, but I wonder why Oscar didn't tell us." *Or
failing that, why Popcorn didn't.*

"My sources"—see above—"indicated that the Chief thinks the Williams-Blackwood case is over and that he doesn't need any, quote, 'amateur help.' But not everybody on the Chief's staff agrees."

"I have no idea who you're talking about, but we appreciate his confidence and thanks for the tip. Do you know when this Hollywood barrister is going to show up in Oscar's office?"

"You and Seb might want to find yourselves there at eleven o'clock this morning. He flew in last night."

"I appreciate this, Aurelia. Got any plans for the holiday?"

"It's so unseasonably warm today that Jack and I are going out to Ramsey Park this afternoon to have a picnic and shoot a few arrows."

I think Cupid's already done that. Keeping that thought to myself, I promised Banfield I wouldn't tell Oscar about the call and wished her many bullseyes. Then I immediately called Mac. He was visiting his old magician friend Septimus Pogue at the Elysian Gardens nursing home that morning but answered quickly. "Good morning, Jefferson," he boomed.

"That remains to be seen."

I filled him in.

"It would be wrong of us to attempt to insert ourselves into Oscar's interview with Mr. Schwartz," he said. "However, he would certainly have no grounds for complaint if we happened to stop by his office to wish him felicitations of the day. I will pick you up."

HOLLY BURDETTE SENT us into Oscar's conference room with a wink and a nod. A criminal justice grad student at SBU, she is smart, ambitious, and knows that Oscar needs her too much to fire her. Hence, her willingness to admit us to the party without an invitation.

Mac opened the door on Oscar sitting across the table from a reasonably good-looking man in his early fifties, with thinning brown hair going gray, a burly build, and tortoise-shell glasses. He looked a little like a myopic bear. "Oh, I am sorry, Oscar," he said, not sounding like it. "I see that you are engaged." He made no effort to move, however.

Oscar looked like he wanted to say, "Don't let the door hit your ass on the way out," but he didn't get that far.

"Are you McCabe?" Oscar's visitor asked.

Mac bowed slightly. "At your service, sir."

"Rufus told me about you. You're supposed to be hot stuff in the sleuthing line, but I haven't seen any evidence of that. I'm Harry Schwartz, Miranda's attorney, here to light a fire under the locals to get these murders solved."

"Hi, I'm Jeff Cody."

Schwartz ignored me.

Speaking of fire, Oscar looked like a rocket about to go off. "Like I was saying," he said, "we have no higher priority than this case, and we have the help of the Ohio Bureau of Criminal Investigation. I believe we know the killer of Parker Williams and Miranda Blackwood, and we've talked to her twice. But it would be a mistake to arrest her before we have enough proof. You can be assured that the BCI will be available to us around the clock to process any evidence of guilt that we uncover."

"Evidence such as what?"

Oscar readjusted his posterior. "Such as whatever we uncover. These things take time."

"The first twenty-four hours are the most important in any murder investigation." As an entertainment lawyer whose criminal experience was probably limited to minor offenses fueled by drugs and alcohol, I was pretty sure he learned that from watching *Midwest Murders* or some similar show. Maybe *The Twenty Most Horrifying Hollywood Murders*.

"Might I ask whether you suspect anyone in Ms. Blackwood's murder?" Mac asked Schwartz.

"I thought you know the killer."

"Chief Hummel and I have a difference of opinion about that."

"Oh, great—Frick and Frack don't agree! Look, it's not my job to finger suspects, but Miranda's murder has to be connected to Williams's, doesn't it?"

"That is the presumption and the most likely scenario," Mac allowed. "However, it has occurred to me that the true connection may not be an obvious one. That is to say, perhaps Ms. Blackwood was the primary victim, even though she was the second."

Schwartz looked puzzled.

"How would that work?"

"Ms. Blackwood inherited Mr. Williams's assets, which are considerable. Whoever inherits from her gets it all."

The lawyer's laugh didn't seem forced. He really thought that was funny. "Some brainstorm! Miranda's estate goes into a trust for Elias, her son. All of it. Every penny."

I wanted to wipe the smirk off his face, so I said, "Not counting your cut for handling the estate. Were you in love with Miranda Blackwood?"

"Of course! I wouldn't have married her otherwise."

Mac gave that one the two raised eyebrows it deserved.

"Married?" Oscar echoed.

Schwartz looked irked at the expressions of surprise. "You heard right. She was my third wife out of four so far, and I was her first husband. Not a lot of people know that, by design. We got married in Vegas right after she finished shooting on her first bit part in a movie and as soon as I could divorce number two. It didn't last long, though. Miranda was very independent and wanted to live her own life—a reaction against her controlling parents, I always thought. Maybe that's why the thing with Parker worked out, him living here and her on the Coast. And it did work out, I have to say that. Whether they were in it for the long haul, who knows. But it was me she trusted with her legal affairs and her son."

He choked up a bit there, paused, then resumed:

"I'm Elias's legal guardian now. He'll be well fixed for the future. Miranda didn't make as much as *Hollywood Reporter* said for the new Red Falcon, but it was a good chunk and a nice slice of the profits to add to the estate. Having handled the prenup, I know that what she inherited from Williams wasn't in that league, but he had some valuable comic book art—including his own."

Mac cleared his throat, a noise that always reminded me of my grandparents' coal furnace kicking on. "We cannot overlook remote possibilities," he said. "Among them is the notion that Ms. Blackwood was the victim of a second killer with a second motive." *What? Where did that come from?* "As one presumably privy to her secrets, do you know of anyone who might hate her enough to kill her?"

The ex-Mr. Blackwood shook his graying head. "No."

"No Hollywood antagonist, such as Winsome Lerouge?"

"Don't be absurd, McCabe."

"I take it, based on your assessment of her marriage, that you think a romantic entanglement by her—with Llewellyn Chase, for example—was unlikely."

"More like impossible."

"That would give him the old 'lover scorned' motive," I pointed out.

"You're not only barking up the wrong tree, you're in the wrong forest," Schwartz said. "Chase has no romantic interest in women." *Red-hot gossip!* "I'm sure you'll find that on the internet somewhere, but he's a voice actor for cartoons and not a big enough name for anybody to notice. I mean, people remember him, but his last live action work was around the time of the first *Star Wars*."

"Well, I guess that's—" Oscar began.

"There is just one more thing," Mac said. He didn't sound like Columbo. "Although I realize that your attorney-client relationship did not end with the death of Ms. Blackwood, I wonder if you would be able to share with us the identity of the father of her son, if you know it."

He gave that a think. "I guess if I answer that it couldn't hurt anything. Fact is, I don't know who the father is, and neither did Miranda. He was a sperm donor. She had all the pertinent information about him—IQ, family medical history, and so forth—but not the name. She didn't want to know. That was part of living her own life. She also got a big kick out of all the tabloid speculation about Elias."

Schwartz stood up. "It's clear to me your so-called investigation is going nowhere fast. I don't believe you have a strong suspect at all. Listen, Miranda Blackwood was more to me than a client. I'm going to make damned sure her killer is caught and put away for good. What levers do I need to pull to make sure that happens? The mayor? The city council?"

Oscar hates dealing with politicians. He also stood, looking Schwartz in the eye. The little beads of sweat on his forehead somewhat undercut this act of mano-a-mano, but he was too pumped to care.

"We're already giving this case everything we've got, Mr. Schwartz."

"Then get more. Or I'll encourage whoever's in charge in this burg to get a new police chief. Is it the mayor? I'm sure they have a campaign fund for the next election."

Chapter Twenty-Eight
Red Herring

"CHEER UP, OSCAR," I advised. "That guy has enough hot air to carry the Wizard's balloon all the way back to Oz."

I was kind of proud of that, but Oscar was unmoved. "Asshole," was his assessment, and I didn't dare ask whether he meant me or Harry Schwartz.

At this point we'd moved down the hall to Oscar's office, where he and Mac were both refueling themselves from Oscar's Keurig machine.

"So where are we now?" I asked the Chief.

"Same as before Asshole came to spread his cheer." *Oh, good, you did mean him.* "Rita Daponte was out to get Williams. She says she's the one who broke off the affair—"

"Long-ago fling," I corrected.

"—but we don't know that's true. Maybe she was still carrying the torch. Anyway, for some reason, she threatened him and eventually carried out the threat. Then a few days later, she entered Williams's house, using a key she kept from when they were fooling around, and searched the place for incriminating evidence. She didn't find it, but you did, Mac. Anyway, Rita Daponte was interrupted by Miranda

Blackwood, giving Mrs. D the unexpected pleasure of killing Williams's wife number three."

"Cogent, but wrong," Mac pronounced. "Jefferson and I have not found anyone who says Mr. Williams feared for his life, and if you had done so you would be shouting it from the rooftops. And Mrs. Daponte is either a far better actress than any others we have encountered in this case, or she is truly remorseful about her dalliance, not regretful that it ended."

"So maybe she figured it was Williams's fault." Oscar uttered this expected speculation with a note of triumph, then downed a slug of coffee.

"Not according to Sister Polly," I said. "And she would know."

"What did Mrs. Daponte say—" Mac began.

There was a knock at Oscar's office door, which was open, followed by Holly Burdette sticking her youthful head in. "Sorry, Chief, thought you'd want to see this guy."

The guy in question, the tall and sandy-haired Gavin Frost-Pierson, brushed past her.

"I want my drawing back," he announced.

"What, no lawyer?" Oscar said.

"I don't need her for this. She told me you found my drawing of The Stinger. I want it back. It proves that I created the character. Besides, it's probably worth a lot of money with all this publicity around the murder."

"Not as much as if you were the one murdered," I offered helpfully.

"I'm afraid you're not getting that sketch back any time soon, if at all, Mr. Frost-Pierson," Oscar said. "It came out of a house that figures in an active murder investigation. Besides, the question of who that piece of paper belongs to is probably going to be argued in court. Your Ms. Snow will be going toe-to-toe with Harry Schwartz and an army of lawyers for the estate. That could take years to sort out."

"I know; that's why I want to cut out the lawyers. The drawing has my initials and some writing on it in my handwriting. It's mine. Just give it to me and I can head back to Akron."

Oscar shook his head. "I can't do that."

"That's not fair!"

Life is like that.

"You seem reluctant to litigate the issue," Mac said. "Could it be that the document in question is of recent vintage, and that you planted it?"

Frost-Pierson exploded. "Why the hell don't people believe me? Well, that doesn't matter. I knew somebody would claim I drew The Stinger just since I started raising a stink about Williams's plagiarism, so I did some investigation. It turns out that the age of documents can be determined by ink chemists and paper experts. We'll call in people like that and they'll prove I'm telling the truth."

The look on Mac's face told me he was mentally thwacking himself upside the head for not thinking of that when he quipped on Wednesday that the document couldn't be carbon-dated. He helped himself to another cup of coffee as he said:

"Of course, it could be argued that even though you created and drew the character you never shared your idea with Parker Williams. However, that would mean that you had to get into the house somehow to leave the drawing where it would be found, most likely on the night of Ms.

Blackwood's murder. We understand from Ms. Snow that you were at home in Akron on Tuesday evening."

"In Akron but not at home," Frost-Pierson said sullenly. "We had a party for Jeffrey, our youngest, at Chuck E. Cheese's with his friends. It was an indulgence. My wife still has a job and, even if she didn't, you want your kid to feel special on his birthday."

"So, plenty of witnesses," Oscar said, just in case Mac and I missed the point.

"I guess so. I saw all the parents at the beginning and end of the party."

"CALL ME SENTIMENTAL, but I feel sorry for the guy," I said after Frost-Pierson left.

"Why?" Oscar grunted.

"I believe him, for one thing. Also, he seems a decent sort with no impulse control who hasn't been very successful." And as I said those words, I was suddenly awash in gratitude for my own life's path. I'd had a solid job ever since graduating with no student loans in 1996 from what was then St. Benignus College. Topping that, I was blessed with a legion of good friends, three adorable kids—and Lynda. Now I felt even sorrier for Gavin Frost-Pierson.

"If he is telling the truth his fortunes may change soon," Mac said. "Most likely Mr. Schwartz will settle quickly on behalf of the Blackwood-Williams estate so as to avoid adverse publicity. Now, back to the matter at hand: Before we were interrupted by that rather dramatic entrance, I was going to ask what Mrs. Daponte said about her fingerprints being in the house."

"Nothing. Erica Slade wouldn't let her talk. But Slade said what you did—that the fingerprints are ancient history. Hey, you didn't give Slade that line, did you?"

"By no means. Would I be correct to gather that the prosecutor remains cautious about proceeding forward on the basis of current evidence?"

"Right. He says the fingerprints aren't enough. I guess he won't be satisfied until we find Daponte's clothes stained with blood from both victims."

"Wait a minute." I sat up, struck by a genius thought. "When you clear away all the brush, don't these two murders leave Harry Schwartz sitting pretty? He's in charge of administering beaucoup bucks for a seven-year-old. That situation is ripe for financial hanky-panky—a million dollars here, a million there, who would notice?"

"Brilliant, Jefferson!" Honest, Mac really said that. And I wholeheartedly agreed. It was one of my best ideas ever. "There are, however, some problems with your theory. First of all, does it really seem to you that Mr. Schwartz could easily disguise himself to the point where his client's husband would not recognize him?"

After a few seconds thought, I said, "He could have hired somebody. So, don't even check to see if he really just flew in from the Left Coast."

"Hiring a professional murderer is no easy task even for an attorney, old boy. And what was the point of the message on the book?"

"A red herring, and a very successful one. It made you take your eyes off the net worth of the two victims. Blackwood had a house in Malibu that will probably be featured in the 'Mansion' section of *The Wall Street Journal* when it sells, and Williams had all that art—notably his own."

"Yes, that art—" Mac stopped. "Yes, art! Why did I not see that?" He thumped his coffee mug on the Chief's desk. "Quite likely, I was wrong, oh so wrong, with my theory that Ms. Blackwood was the principal victim. No, these murders are all about art. Not forged art, but the real thing— Parker Williams's Red Falcon art."

"You want to slow walk this for me, Mac?" Oscar suggested.

"There is a question I often ask in criminous matters, and which I regrettably neglected to ask this time: What did the murder change? Not just who benefited—the famous *cui bono,* which may not be clear—but *what has changed.* In this case, one of the answers is that Mr. Williams's art is almost certainly worth much more now that he is dead. As we have heard repeatedly over the past week, that often happens upon an artist's demise. Jefferson alluded to the phenomenon with his flip comment a few moments ago to Mr. Frost-Pierson that his art would be worth even more if he were dead."

I would say "clever," not "flip."

Oscar shrugged. "So what? Any original artwork that he still had is part of his estate."

"Of course. However, most of the art that Parker Williams created was no longer his—it was sold. Or even given away, especially before he became a collectable artist. I have a notion that I would like to confirm by another visit to the Williams studio."

"What do you expect to find there?"

"If I am correct, nothing."

OSCAR AND OFFICER Lehmann went along to help give the studio a good going-over. And what were we looking for?

"Writing on the edge of a book," Mac said.

"What book?" Lehmann asked.

"Any book."

About thirty minutes later, the verdict was in.

"Nothing, Chief," Lehmann reported, which made it unanimous. The only book with writing on the edge in that book-clogged room was *Red Harvest*.

"That is because, as I have long believed, the 'I fear RED' message was a red herring in the truest sense—a false path down which the killer led us," Mac said.

"So, who's the killer?" Lehmann asked.

Instead of answering, Mac addressed Oscar: "You have Gavin Frost-Pierson's phone number? Good. He should not be far out of town by now, or perhaps he has even stopped for lunch or to visit Ms. Snow. Ask him to meet us at 2852 Rachel's Way at five o'clock. I have a few corners of this case to nail down before then."

"Rachel's Way—Williams's house, you mean."

"Yes. And ask Mr. Frost-Pierson—tell him—to bring his attorney. Assistant Chiefs Gibbons and Banfield may wish to be present as well. Mr. and Mrs. Daponte, along with Sarah-Jane Manders and Harry Schwartz will round out the group nicely."

"Can I come, too?"

Mac ignored Oscar's jibe. "I suppose you want me to explain. Very well, then. That will take a few minutes, so please make those calls first."

"So, you don't want to hold up the party so that Rufus, Spargo, Post, or one of the actors can get back to town and join us?" I asked.

"No, Jefferson, the seeds of these murders were home-grown."

Chapter Twenty-Nine
The Woman in Red

"THIS PLACE HASN'T changed much since the last time I saw it," Felicity Snow said, looking around Parker Williams's studio in the house that had once been her home.

"I am not surprised," Mac said.

"Why am I here?" her client demanded.

"Because you, Mr. Frost-Pierson, are a key player in the drama that will end in this room in a few moments." *Don't be so dramatic.* "Let us begin with the obvious fact that Parker Williams's dying message, composed of the words 'woman' and 'red,' referred to the gender and the hair color of his assailant."

"Obvious!" Banfield exploded. "Isn't the meaning of 'the woman in red' what we've been trying to figure out all along, Seb?" Apparently, Gibbons—who knew what was up—hadn't filled her in on the end game when he called and invited her to the soiree. Maybe he wanted to surprise her. Or maybe they had other things to talk about. Anyway, Mac, Oscar, Gibbons, and I were the only ones in the studio who knew where this was going. Gibbons remained quiet for most of what followed, clutching an Ohio Association of Chiefs of Police tote bag.

"Not quite," Mac answered Banfield. "The killer was indeed a woman, but not *in* red. She was *with* red—that is, with red hair. As I explained to Jefferson recently, clothing, jewelry, or anything of that sort would not be a clue a dying man would fix on—it does not narrow the field enough. Nor would a red costume mean anything at a comic book expo full of them. Red hair, on the other hand, is relatively rare despite what I understand is a current vogue for dyeing hair that color. The number of redheads might have been in the triple digits in a crowd this size, as the coroner observed, but it was still a limiting factor."

This was going to get very complicated very fast, which is why I promised Lynda that I would record it all on my phone for Johanna to use in writing her story about Sebastian McCabe's latest rabbit-from-a-hat. Tall Rawls wasn't invited to this party, maybe because of limited space. Harry Schwartz came but looked highly peeved about it. Rita Daponte seemed nervous, fingering her crucifix, and Al held her hand supportively. Sara-Jane Manders just looked puzzled with a "why am I here?" expression on her face.

"Where did the phrase 'woman in red' come from anyway?" Mac asked rhetorically.

"The *Observer*," Snow said. "It was a big headline."

Mac shook his head. "That is not where it started. The phrase originated with an uninvited collaborator on this case, an amateur online sleuth called Bethany Lane. I have long been convinced this was a pseudonym because it is the name of a street here in Erin, near the Silk Stocking Winery. And now I am convinced that false name hides the killer of Parker Williams and Miranda Blackwood. The 'woman in red' phrase was the first red herring of the case, one designed to steer us away from the true meaning of Mr. Williams's dying message. That is why in one of Bethany Lane's posts about the case she gave a long list of possible meanings of 'red' without mentioning the obvious possibility of hair, as I observed to Jefferson."

"So the killer was a red-haired woman," Snow said, just to be clear.

"No, not at all."

Rita Daponte wasn't the only one to gape at that. And her husband said a word I don't use in these chronicles, although a lot of movies do. "Based on potential motives," Mac continued, "there was only one serious suspect who had red hair, and graying at that—I refer to Mr. Red O'Connor, who was not a woman. The 'red' in Mr. Williams's message could have referred to Mr. O'Connor by name or by hair color, but not if he were in disguise as a woman. After all, it is unlikely that he would dress as a woman and wear a wig of the same fading color of his own hair. Therefore, I concluded that the killer was a woman wearing a red wig or, less likely but still possible, a man in a wig dressed as a woman."

"Concluded?" Frost-Pierson echoed. "You mean speculated." I hope he was that careful with words in his journalistic writing.

"If you wish. However, my speculation was correct. More about that later. For now—"

"Wait a minute," Harry Schwartz interrupted, being a lawyer. "Why would the killer try to steer law enforcement away from the idea that the killer was a redhead if the hair was a wig?"

"She could have been afraid of having been seen in the red hair," Mac speculated. "However, I suspect she was fearful of the police launching a search for the wig, realizing that it may hold clues to her identity."

"For a guy who thought he was so smart, Parker didn't leave a very good clue," Sarah-Jane Manders said.

Mac nodded. "Indeed, he did not. He merely wrote what he saw, which was not helpful. We must not be too critical, however; Mr. Williams was in the process of dying at the time. At any rate, I had to solve"—Oscar, having promised to let Mac lead this circus, scowled—"that is to say, in my capacity as an advisor to Chief Hummel, I had to work my way to a suggestion about the killer's identity through motive, and then prove opportunity. I believe I know the means as well, although that will have to await the search warrant that is in the Chief's pocket."

"Wait a minute," Daponte said. "How do you know the murderer even had a good motive? Maybe she was just nutso."

"No one has a good motive for murder, Mr. Daponte. I only looked for a rational one; an irrational one would be beyond the scope of discovery. I did that by asking myself, far too late, what changed as a result of Mr. Williams's murder. Death changes many things, of course, but in the case of an artist it almost inevitably means that the deceased's work is more valuable, assuming it had any value at all to begin with. This is not an arcane fact. Jefferson tells me that it was even the subject of a *Wall Street Journal* story not so very long ago and has been mentioned by several individuals in our discussions over the past ten days.

"This murder was not about love, but money. Who, then, benefited financially by the death of Parker Williams causing his artwork to be more valuable?"

"Not me!" Frost-Pierson exclaimed.

Almost simultaneously, Schwartz burst out with, "You're going to say Miranda! But then who killed *her*—Elias?"

"Although Ms. Blackwood is the obvious beneficiary of her husband's death, that is irrelevant. There is another woman whom I erred in thinking did not profit from his demise—Parker Williams's first wife, Ms. Snow."

"Felicity?" That was Manders, Snow's friend and fellow ex-spouse.

"You!" Rita Daponte said to Snow, making it sound like a curse word.

Everybody in the room stared at Snow, who stared at Mac. None of them looked more sucker-punched than Frost-Pierson.

Banfield was the first to recover. "I give up, Seb. How did she profit?"

"I want to hear this myself," Snow said with a fair imitation of surprise, outrage, and innocence. Maybe she should have been an actor, although a courtroom attorney is pretty much the same thing.

"And, of course, you shall hear it," Mac said. "First, let me take the liberty of setting the stage a bit, Ms. Snow. You are a late bloomer as an attorney, still burdened with large debt like so many professionals today. In fact, in an interview with Assistant Chiefs Gibbons and Banfield you referred to 'all that student loan debt.' You share office space with a small firm and are engaged to a teacher who I have established does not himself have large financial resources. In other words, you could use money—especially since your friend Ms. Manders here told us that you received little out of your marriage to Parker Williams in terms of a settlement because he had not yet become successful when you parted."

"Thanks," Snow told Manders. But the latter was paying too close attention to Mac to defend herself for this indiscretion. Mac ignored her, too, and went on, addressing the others:

"And yet, there is something of value we might surmise that Mr. Williams gave his first spouse before they divorced. The facial similarity between Ms. Snow and Red Falcon is unmistakable even when the character is wearing a mask. Ms. Snow herself acknowledged that she was the physical model for the character. How likely is it that the artist would have given her one of those early drawings at the time he executed it, while the two were still married? Quite likely. And how likely is it that she would have kept it as a memento, or perhaps simply stuck it somewhere and rediscovered it recently? Perhaps not quite as likely, but reasonably so. Any such art would be worth a substantial sum of money, given the popularity of the character—but far more if the artist were dead."

"And if that weren't obvious, she would have read about it in that *Wall Street Journal* story a few weeks ago," I blurted out, having seen the *WSJ* on Snow's messy desk when we visited her office.

"How it must have galled her knowing that Parker Williams had, in a sense, stolen her image and continued to profit from it. I suspect that a look at the search history on her computer would show that she researched the prices of original comic artwork. Perhaps she thought of selling the art immediately to raise money, but then thought 'if only he were dead.' And from the thought sprang action."

"Is that all you have?" Snow was controlled, lawyerly.

"*Au contraire*, I have only started."

"Then I'm going to stop you. You seem to have forgotten that I was in Cincinnati shopping and eating until after four o'clock on the day of the murder and I have a parking receipt to prove it."

"The spuriousness of that alibi is but another indication of your guilt, Ms. Snow. I talked to your fiancé, Bob Cartwright—"

"You bastard!"

"—and through a subterfuge of which I am not proud, I was able to establish that on the day in question you called him in late morning and asked him to pick you up in Cincinnati and bring you back to Erin because your car had died. Later—immediately after the murder, in fact—he took you back to Cincinnati, where you insisted that he leave you in front of an auto repair shop. In reality, you walked from there to the lot where you had left your car. The mere fact that you lied earlier and again today about being in Cincinnati until after four o'clock that day condemns you. So would cell phone tracking. You have nothing to say?"

Snow gave a crooked smile. "My lawyer advised me against it." She turned to Oscar. "Shouldn't you Mirandize me?"

"Not yet—you aren't in custody," he reminded her.

"I don't believe this," Frost-Pierson said. But he did. The look on his face screamed that.

"What about the second murder, the one I was accused of?" Rita Daponte asked, with a dagger-glance at Oscar.

"I am just arriving at that," Mac said. "Your fingerprints are in this house, Ms. Daponte, and so are those of Mr.

Williams's wives—including, of course, Ms. Snow. Miranda Blackwood noted that her husband lived in this house 'forever' and that she was the third 'lady of the house,' although she never actually lived here. Some people may change the locks in a home they continue to occupy after a divorce, knowing that the former spouse has a key. I will wager, however, that Mr. Williams did not. That would explain the lack of forced entry here by the killer."

"I don't have a key," Snow said. "You can search my purse." She held it up, a modest-sized handbag that was black, not red.

"That will not be necessary. You would scarcely have been foolish enough to retain it."

"Why?" Schwartz said. "Why kill Miranda?" He packed a lot of heat into those few words.

"The most obvious answer to that question turns out to be true: She interrupted the killer. The ironic blow with a Red Falcon statue that took Ms. Blackwood's life was the unpremeditated act that it seemed. However, the victim did not interrupt a search of the home, as it first appeared. She disturbed Ms. Snow in the act of planting the false message 'I fear RED.' That message was designed to end the search for Parker Williams's murderer by simultaneously appearing to support his dying words—the existence of which kept the search for the killer very much alive both in fact and in the public imagination—and also point directly to a plausible killer, Rita Ellison Daponte.

"However, that false clue turned back on you, Ms. Snow. When Chief Hummel elected to keep the message secret, you attempted without success to get Johanna Rawls at the *Observer* to report it. Failing that, as 'Bethany Lane' you not only publicized the message, you pushed the narrative that it referred to Rita Daponte. That was a mistake. At one point Erica Slade asked us, 'And who calls my client "Rita Ellison Daponte" anyway?' The answer is you. You did so during an interview with the two assistant chiefs, Jefferson, and me. So, you knew Mrs. Daponte's three initials, and you also had great animus toward her."

"You mean she hated her?" Banfield asked. "Why?"

"Because of Ms. Manders."

"Me!" The tattoo artist's surprise seemed the real deal to me.

"By her own testimony and yours, you two were friends. Ms. Snow resented Ms. Daponte's affair with Mr. Williams on your behalf. That is why you, Ms. Snow, planted the false clue implicating Rita Daponte and directed us to it by encouraging me to search this home, purportedly for evidence of your client's plagiarism claims. You also said that your ex-husband had a habit of drawing on the sides of books, leading me to look there. However, an examination of hundreds of volumes here this afternoon showed that was not the case. That proved to my satisfaction that the only such writing was done by you."

And that was it. Mac had emptied his whole bag of tricks. We didn't expect Felicity Snow to crumble, and she didn't.

"I would call all of that circumstantial evidence except that it's not evidence," she said. "I can explain everything, and I will at the appropriate time and place."

As soon as I come up with it, she might as well have said.

And then Gibbons dropped the big one, showing an unexpected sense of drama.

"I have something to add." He put on nitrile gloves and reached into his Ohio Association of Chiefs of Police tote bag to bring out a bright red wig of shoulder-length. "After several days of searching, Officer Mentzel found it this afternoon in a dumpster on Broadway, several blocks down from SBU Towne Center. It contained three dark hairs which belonged to the person who wore this wig, and the BCI will be able to establish that person's identity through DNA."

Mac and I didn't know any of that, but Oscar did. I'm sure he controlled the look of satisfaction on his broad face only with great effort as he said: "That should be enough evidence to satisfy the prosecutor. I'm taking you into custody, Ms. Snow. You have the right to remain silent . . ."

Chapter Thirty
Red Carpet

GIBBONS WAS RIGHT about the hair in the wig being traced back to Felicity Snow by the DNA. So, in the end, even though Williams's "WOMAN RED" didn't lead to the killer, it did help to prove the killer.

And that wasn't the only DNA evidence. Parker Williams's blood was on a curved boning knife found under search warrant in the kitchen of the apartment Snow shared with Bob Cartwright. That stuff just doesn't wash off. The knife was a six-inch Victorinox Swiss Army Cutlery Fibrox which garnered 733 reviews and five stars on Amazon.

"Sarah-Jane told us she and Felicity rebonded over 'those gourmet meals she cooks up,'" I said to Lynda one evening at cocktail hour during the trial. "That's why she had the knife."

She shivered. "Why didn't she get rid of it?"

"Mac thinks she was afraid that Bob Cartwright would notice it was missing."

"I feel sorry for him. He seems like a decent guy, from what I hear."

Cartwright was certainly loyal. He stood by Snow throughout the trial, taking time off from teaching to appear in court every day.

Phoebe Farleigh's best game wasn't enough to keep Snow from being convicted of two counts of first-degree murder—Williams's qualifying for that charge because of premeditation, and Blackwood's because it happened during the commission of a robbery. Snow picked Farleigh for her defense because she shared office space with the Farleigh & Farleigh firm. I'm not sure that even Erica Slade, ably assisted by her paralegal and Poisoned Pens member Ashley Crutcher, could have done any better. But when the judge dished out two life sentences instead of the seldom-imposed death penalty, I think Farleigh should have declared victory and gone home. Instead, she appealed—to no avail.

Winter moved into spring, the pandemic continued to ebb as variants got more contagious but less serious, and daylight saving time returned. Mac's self-confidence, battered by the English garden case, also returned; you might call that a mixed blessing.

One day in May 2023, more than a year after the murders, Mac and I made the two-and-a-half-hour drive to visit Felicity Snow at the Ohio Reformatory for Women in Marysville. They call it a reformatory, but it's a prison. We'd been there before, visiting the killer of an SBU employee.[17] That was a corporal work of mercy; this time Mac wanted to tidy up some loose ends.

Snow rolled out the red carpet for us, by which I mean she agreed to talk and answer questions truthfully. Her hair was pinned back, and the prison uniform wasn't especially fetching.

"No hard feelings," she assured us. "But you were wrong about a lot of things, McCabe."

---

[17] See *Too Many Clues* (MX Publishing, 2019).

He raised an eyebrow. "Such as?"

"For starters, you said the murder wasn't about love but money. In a way, it was about love—my love for Bob. I didn't want to saddle him with my student debt when we got married. There's been some loan forgiveness since that day last February, but not enough to help me much. And that's okay, I was an adult when I chose to take on the obligation. But Bob didn't make that choice. He still visits me every week, you know. I want him to move on, but he won't. I think he feels guilty about busting my alibi. I should just refuse to see him, but I don't have the heart to let him down again."

Contrary to form, Mac said nothing.

"By the way, McCabe, there was no great master plan except to stab Parker when no one was looking and try not to get caught. I picked the Expo to do it because there were so many people around no one would ever know I was there—especially since I had the parking receipt for an alibi and the wig for a disguise. I also dressed in loose clothing that didn't show my body shape, unlike those superhero costumes.

"I didn't see Parker in the first half-hour or so that I was at the Towne Center, so I decided to take the elevator upstairs. And when the elevator doors opened, there he was. Alone. He didn't recognize me, so I got in the elevator and stabbed him quickly before I lost my nerve. Then I pushed the elevator button and got off, terrified because I knew somebody could come along any second, even though the hallway outside the elevator was empty."

"You got lucky," I said.

She shook her head. "No, I didn't. If I'd been caught right then I'd still be here in prison and Miranda Blackwood, who never did me any harm, would be alive."

"Why the red wig?" Mac asked.

"It wasn't just a wig. I also wore a red scarf. The idea was that if anybody saw me, that's what they would remember. I wasn't trying to fool Parker; he'd be dead."

"Why not just wear a protective face mask?"

"I don't believe in them." She leaned forward. "I've never handled criminal work, but everybody knows that a killer can't profit by the crime. Do you think the value added to Parker's early Red Falcon counts?"

Mac shrugged his massive shoulders. "I hesitate to say. That will be up to a court, I suppose, and courts are unfathomable."

"I'd like to sell it to pay my debts and then give the rest, if there is any, to Bob."

THAT WAS JUST the other day.

Not long ago, Popcorn called my attention to a story that Rasputin Spargo was the successful bidder for the inaugural *She-Wolf* cover art once owned by the late artist-writer Parker Williams. The back story dredged up the murder, and also mentioned that the director of the Library & Museum of Popular Culture profusely apologized for exhibiting a forgery. Red O'Connor stepped forward to admit being the forger, which caused his career to take off again. He's riding the Comic Book Expo circuit in bigger cities now and executing commissions out the wazoo. And . . .

"Kyle Rufus went to work for Winsome Lerouge," Kelly Richards informed me one day.

"Who keeps track of that?"

"TMZ. Not that they report on PAs as a usual thing, but their story today about the *Queen Bee* movie did a deep dive on everybody involved in the Williams-Blackwood murders. Oh, and Lynda's old beau Gavin Frost-Pierson gets credited as the creator of Queen Bee, both in the movie and in any future comics. Not only that, apparently the recognition has re-ignited his creative juices and he's got new projects in the works with Paragon Comics."

"I wouldn't call him an old beau."

That long-awaited *Queen Bee* flick had been delayed in post-production but is just about to hit the screens, both big and little. Lynda and Triple M can't wait to see it. I told them they can make it a girls' night out. I've had enough of super-villains.

A Few Words of Thanks

This is where I get to shout out to the members of Team Cody, those selfless souls who do the hard work of fixing all my errors of spelling, grammar, facts, and plot:

Ann Brauer Andriacco, for putting up with this writer—the dedication page says it all;

Michael Andriacco, the true creator of some of the comic book characters within these pages, for his super-hero/supervillain savvy;

Peg Hausman, an old friend but the newest team member, for her expert copyediting;

Jeff Suess, for providing invaluable insight into the world of comic books, graphic novels, and comic expos, as well as his usual beta reading; and

Steve Winter, yet again, for giving the second draft the incredible benefit of his engineering eye and making dozens of helpful suggestions.

Any errors that remain are mine, not theirs. And for the record, the Red Falcon and Queen Bee in this book are not to be confused with characters of those names who exist, existed, or might ever exist in this or any other universe.

Publisher Steve Emecz and cover illustrator Brian Belanger are the easiest collaborators any writer was ever so lucky to have. MX Publishing is a social enterprise venture that is both enterprising and venturesome.

About the Author

Dan Andriacco has been reading mysteries since he discovered Sherlock Holmes at the age of about nine and writing them almost as long. His first published work, however, was a Sherlock Holmes pastiche short story in 1990. The McCabe-Cody series began in 2011.

After almost 24 years as a reporter and business editor of a daily newspaper, Dan served as communications director for a religious nonprofit for 20 years. He holds a master's degree in religion and a doctorate in ministry.

A Baker Street Irregular ("St. Saviour's Near King's Cross"), Dan is the Most Scandalous Member (leader) of the Tankerville Club of Cincinnati and a member of numerous other scion societies of the BSI. He also wears bow ties. You can follow his long-running blog at www.danandriacco.com and his Facebook Fan Page, Dan Andriacco Mysteries.

Dan and his partner in criminous endeavors, Ann Brauer Andriacco, have three grown children and six grandchildren. They live in Cincinnati, Ohio, USA, about forty miles downriver from the town of Erin, which is located on no map.

Also from MX Publishing

Visit www.mxpublishing.com for dozens of other Sherlock Holmes novels, novellas, short story collections, Conan Doyle biographies, Holmes travel books, and more.

London-based MX Publishing is the award-winning, world's largest independent Sherlock Holmes Book publisher, with hundreds of books in print. Follow MX—

On Facebook:
https://www.facebook.com/BooksSherlockHolmes/

On Twitter:
https://twitter.com/mxpublishing

On Instagram:
https://www.instagram.com/mxpublishing/

www.ingramcontent.com/pod-product-compliance
Lightning Source LLC
Chambersburg PA
CBHW070104280626
47159CB00016B/1183